# FATE IN FREEFALL

Paralysed by grief after losing her fiancé in a skydiving accident, Katrina Maslow cannot allow herself to love another man. She travels the world in an attempt to flee from her former life, ending up in Rio and accepting a job as a guide with J Stone Adventure Trips. But Jay, the handsome owner of the company, is determined to break down her reserves. As they are pursued by a ruthless killer, Katrina finally realises she is in love with Jay — just at the moment she might lose him forever . . .

KEN PRESTON

# FATE IN FREEFALL

*Complete and Unabridged*

LINFORD
*Leicester*

First published in Great Britain in 2013



First Linford Edition
published 2014



*A catalogue record for this book is available from the British Library.*

ISBN 978–1–4448–2082–9

Published by
F. A. Thorpe (Publishing)
Anstey, Leicestershire

Set by Words & Graphics Ltd.
Anstey, Leicestershire
Printed and bound in Great Britain by
T. J. International Ltd., Padstow, Cornwall

This book is printed on acid-free paper

# Prologue

## Somewhere over Kent, England

'Okay, everyone, listen up! Twenty seconds to freefall!'

Katrina smiled as she watched her students check their harnesses one final time. Parachute integrity checks had already been performed on the ground. With only twenty seconds to spare before departing the aircraft, this was no time for a detailed safety inspection. Instead, it was one last chance to check their parachute packs were strapped on securely, and then get ready to jump into the void.

This was Katrina's favourite moment, just before a skydive. She was knotted up with tension and exhilaration, her muscles twitching with adrenaline. No matter how many times she jumped, it was always in these final moments, just before she stepped out of the door to fall through the air, that she felt truly alive. Did it say something about her character, that she had to court death to feel as though she was living?

Some people spent Sunday afternoons going for walks in the countryside. Others collected stamps, or painted pictures of pretty landscapes in watercolours, or read a book. Not Katrina. No; here she was, about to leap from a plane, 12,000 feet above sea level, risking her survival on a carefully packed expanse of nylon and string strapped to her back.

Many of her friends and family thought she was a little bit crazy, and sometimes Katrina wondered if they were right. But Pete understood her — was driven by the same need for excitement, and that adrenaline rush that only came when leaping into the void.

Katrina sometimes thought about what it would be like to make that leap without a parachute. Of course, that would be suicide, and Katrina wasn't the suicidal type. But still, she couldn't help but wonder how that would feel.

And there was always the possibility that her parachute would fail to open — that instead of billowing out, unfolding and filling with air to arrest her fall, it would flap around in a useless tangle just over her head, leaving her to plunge to the ground.

Katrina knew this was unlikely, and that she had her reserve parachute in case of any such disasters. But still, the fear lingered — a natural instinct, considering she was about to leap into thin air and freefall for a full minute before opening her parachute.

The roar of the plane's engine deepened as they slowed to cruising speed. She glanced across at Pete, who smiled and blew her a kiss. This was to be their last jump as an unmarried couple. In two days' time they were going to declare their love and commitment for one another in a lavish ceremony in front of family and friends.

Katrina had never been happier. She had met Pete when she was first learning to skydive, and he was her tutor. He had taught her everything she knew, and now she was an instructor too. They had been together five years, content with their lives, with no thoughts of marriage. Then, one sunny Sunday morning in the spring, Pete had started talking about having children.

'Neither of us is getting any younger, you know,' he said, lying next to her in bed, propped up on one elbow, running his fingers through her hair with his free hand. She loved it when he did this, sometimes wishing he would never stop. And to Katrina, he had never looked more handsome, as the sunlight streamed through the bedroom windows, bathing him a warm glow.

She laughed. 'Isn't this a bit back-to-front? I thought it was the woman who was supposed to nag the man for kids?'

'Don't you want kids?' Pete raised an eyebrow, as if to say, *Come on, I know you better than that*.

Katrina gazed into Pete's eyes and thought, *I can't believe I — this is the man I'm going to spend the rest of my life with.*

'Of course I want kids,' she whispered, running her fingers down his cheek. 'It's just . . . not the right time yet.'

Pete pulled a face, full of mock disbelief. 'So when will be the right time?'

'I don't know. Like, when we're married?'

Pete sat up, the bedclothes dropping from his torso. 'Then let's get married! Come on, Katrina, let's do it!' He jumped out of bed, naked, and knelt on the floor beside her. 'Katrina Maslow, will you do me the great honour of being my wife? Please?'

Katrina giggled. 'I wonder how many girls have been proposed to by a naked man before.'

'As long as you don't make me ask your parents for their permission to marry you, in the nude.'

Laughing, Katrina slid out of bed, naked too, and wrapped her arms around Pete. 'Of course I'll marry you.'

She kissed him. 'And then let's start a family.'

Pete kissed her back. 'Hmm, I think I'm suddenly feeling the urge to start a family right now!'

* * *

Now here they were, 12,000 feet in the air, ready to jump for the last time before becoming Mr and Mrs Sullivan. What made today's jump even more special was that one of Katrina's students, Jo, was also her best friend, and she was going to be her bridesmaid on Saturday.

Katrina glanced over at Jo and stuck her thumbs up. Jo gave her a bright, excited smile.

'Okay everybody, let's line up!' Pete stood up, and the five students followed his example. None of them were complete novices, but this was their first time jumping from this height. Pete opened the door, the cabin suddenly filling with gusts of wind, the engine noise now deafeningly loud. Pete stood by the door, the students shuffling into a line behind him, and Katrina joined them at the back. Talk was almost impossible now; everything had to be done by hand signals.

Pete raised a hand and gave them all the thumbs up. Then he turned his back to them and stepped through the open door. One after another each of the students leaped after him, following their instructions exactly. They were all going to try and form a circle by linking hands as they fell. Once out of the door each skydiver had a minute before they needed to pull the ripcord, so speed was of the essence. Everyone had to act immediately, with complete conviction. When hurtling towards solid ground at speeds of 130 miles per hour, there was no place for indecision.

Katrina stood at the door, a patchwork quilt of greens and browns in the distance below her. The ground suddenly seemed unreal from up here, almost as though it was an optical illusion. The young woman hesitated for only a fraction of a second before launching herself into space.

Once out of the aircraft her nerves disappeared, replaced by excitement and total, overwhelming joy. Automatically she extended her arms out to her sides and arched her back, the effect of which was to slow her downwards velocity. She began counting down the seconds from sixty to zero. The wind battered her face, pulling at her goggles and the strands of hair set free from her helmet.

Up here, she felt like Superman, like she was flying. At these moments, Katrina could not understand why so many of her friends refused to even try skydiving. It was simply the best feeling in the world. Falling through the atmosphere at 130 miles per hour, Katrina felt invincible — as though she could take on anyone and anything, and win.

She twisted and turned, looking for the others. Pete had already linked up with three of the students, the circle half-formed. The other three were rapidly closing in. Katrina felt a rush of pride, watching as their students performed to perfection.

Fifty seconds left.

Katrina knew she had to get moving. As the last one out of the plane she would be the last link in the circle. She angled herself, dipping her head and shoulders, straightening her back and pushing her arms into her sides, so increasing her rate of fall. As she fell closer to the others, two more students linked hands as the final student approached.

Forty seconds left.

The ground still appeared to be a great distance away, giving the illusion that they were flying, not falling. Katrina knew from experience that this would change at a moment's notice. Optical illusion suddenly gives way to reality, and the ground begins rushing upwards at an alarming rate.

Thirty seconds left.

The final student linked up with his fellow skydiver on his right, and then

Katrina was there too, linking hands with the people on her right and left.

They'd done it!

Katrina looked at each of the faces in turn, all of them smiling, laughing, eyes alight with excitement. She felt so proud of them all. Jo, who was looking back at Katrina, was grinning so happily that Katrina's face muscles began to hurt as she smiled even more. Finally, she let her gaze fall on Pete. He mouthed the words 'I love you', as they flew through the air, over the English countryside. Katrina experienced an overpowering surge of love for this man she was going to create a family with, a love so powerful her insides ached with it.

She was the happiest person in the whole world.

Pete let go, breaking the circle, and began drifting away, sticking both thumbs up. His departure was the signal for the rest of the group to break apart and spread out, ready to deploy their parachutes.

Ten seconds to go.

Katrina positioned herself, spreading

out her arms and legs again, slowing her rate of descent as much as possible. She needed to do this to reduce the impact on her body as the parachute opened, and dramatically slowed her rate of fall, from 130 to only 13 miles per hour. It was this sudden braking that gave inexperienced skydivers the sensation of being pulled upwards when their parachute opened.

A last quick look around, to make sure she was out of everybody's space, and then she gripped the ripcord.

Zero seconds.

Katrina pulled on the ripcord and felt the parachute unfolding behind and above her. A moment later and she struggled to catch her breath as she was seemingly yanked upward by an invisible, giant hand. Her speed of descent decreased suddenly, the harness straining against her torso as her body tried to continue downward at its previous, freefalling rate.

Katrina looked around and saw everyone floating safely to earth, the bright orange parachutes a beautiful contrast against the deep blue sky. Then she looked down and saw one of their group still hurtling to the ground. Her insides turned over as she realised it was Pete. His parachute had only partially opened, and was flapping in a tangled mess just over his head.

'Open your reserve 'chute!' she screamed as he plunged earthwards. 'Open your reserve!'

Helpless, she watched as Pete's body grew smaller and smaller, rushing to meet the approaching ground. She closed her eyes at the last moment, arching her head back and screaming his name.

Katrina struggled in her harness as she floated to earth, wanting to get down as quickly as possible. She landed in a flurry of arms and legs. The parachute billowed down and enveloped her before she had a chance to move out of its way. Not at all the textbook landing she had perfected, and taught others all these years. She scrambled to her feet, the parachute trapping her like a net. Panicking, she began pulling at the nylon, searching for a gap, an exit point.

She had to get to Pete. Somehow, miraculously, he could still be alive. It was possible. There were lots of stories of people surviving falls from incredible heights, many of them without a parachute at all.

He had to be alive. He had to be!

Katrina managed to extricate herself and unclipped her harness. Every one of the skydivers was safely down now. Some of them were already free of their parachutes and were running over to find Pete. Katrina stumbled after them, her legs trembling and weak, her insides churning with fear.

'Please let him be alive, please God, let him be alive,' she cried as she stumbled through the field.

A body collided with her, arms wrapping around her, pinning her in place. Jo, holding her, crying.

'Stay here, Kat, please stay here. It's too late,' she sobbed. 'He's dead, Kat. He's dead.'

'No! He can't be!' Katrina struggled

against her friend's tight embrace. Other students were surrounding her now, reaching out to her, crying. Katrina knew she had to free herself. She had see Pete with her own eyes.

*He can't be dead! This isn't happening!*

Katrina's world grew first grey, and then black. She felt herself falling into the darkness, before oblivion swallowed her up in its cold embrace.

# 1

## Two Years Later, Rio de Janeiro

Oliver Lowenstein pops another of his daily regimen of pills, and chases it down with the last of his iced tea. Lowenstein has eight different sets of pills he has to take every day. Pills for his diabetes, blood pressure, angina, for his thyroid, pills to help him sleep, pills to wake him up — the list sometimes seems not only endless, but pointless.

Once he had been fit and healthy, young and indestructible. Now, it seems, his body has become a receptacle for an excess of medication, the intention being to keep him alive. Soon, Lowenstein feels, he will stop taking the medicine, and let nature take its course.

But not yet. He has something important to accomplish first.

The waitress smiles as she brings him

another iced tea. His bladder will soon be protesting at all this drinking, but Lowenstein does not care. Surely, at his age, he should be allowed his little luxuries?

The professor returns the waitress's smile. Body language is the only form of communication they share. He is British and she, he presumes, speaks only Portuguese. The barrier of language is like a brick wall between them. Lowenstein feels as though he is in a prison of his own making in this country. He has no knowledge of its language, or customs, or its currency. He feels trapped in a cocoon of stupidity. For a scientist, a man who collects data and information like others collect stamps or comic books, who appreciates the value of learning and the power of knowledge, living in ignorance like this is a form of torture.

Sipping his drink, Lowenstein sits in his window seat and regards the massive, colourful display on the front of the building across the busy forecourt.

Rio 2016: World Climate Conference.

This is why he is here, braving foreign languages and customs. To try and avert a worldwide disaster in the making. A disaster born of greed and profit margins. If he can accomplish this one thing, then his conscience will be clean once more. He can go home and live at peace with himself, spending the rest of his days in his Cornish cottage by the sea, surrounded by memories of his wife and their long, happy marriage.

Lowenstein stiffens as he watches the man weaving through the crowds and approaching the café. His face and arms are darkly suntanned, his body muscular, his head shaven and his eyes hidden by wraparound sunglasses. He is wearing jeans and a short-sleeved, colourful shirt, his armpits darkened with circles of sweat.

The cup rattles against the saucer as the scientist puts it down. Lowenstein has never met this man, but he has seen him before. The man has been following him ever since Lowenstein arrived in Rio, the scientist is positive of that. And he knows the man has come to kill him.

Professor Lowenstein is an old man, and has lived most of his life in the laboratory, or at the front of a lecture hall. To find himself, at his advanced age, caught in the middle of events that could have come out of a Hollywood thriller, seems ridiculous to him. And yet the danger, he knows, is all too real.

Lowenstein stands up, his iced tea unfinished, and tips unfamiliar coins onto the table. As he leaves by the rear exit, he regrets his unfamiliarity with the local currency, and hopes that he has left enough of a tip for the smiling waitress.

* * *

'Hey, Quinn, get yourself out here and start going through these accounts, will ya?' Jay shouts, sitting down and planting a thick wad of bills and invoices on the desk.

Quintessence Jackson struts into the office, in a short T-shirt and cut-off jeans, and lobs a screwed-up ball of paper at Jay. 'Well if you'd get your lily-white, bony ass out of my chair, maybe I could do some work!'

'Okay, okay,' Jay laughs, jumping out of the chair and fending off another paper missile.

'And maybe you kids don't get taught manners Down Under, but here in Rio, we says our pleases and our thank yous.' She stands there, feet spread and hands on hips, and Jay can't help but admire the fine figure she cuts. But a little scary, also.

'You're right, I'm sorry.' He grins and shrugs.

Quinn strides across the room and plants herself in her chair, looks up at Jay, and laughs. 'No need, Outback Guy.'

Jay pops his head through the door, where Quinn was watching the tiny television bolted to the wall in the waiting room. On the screen, protesters with placards are milling around a cavalcade of black limousines.

'What's happening out there, anyway?'

'They're protesting about climate change,' Quinn says, swinging her feet up onto the desk.

'What, they're for it or against it?'

'Against it, you idiot.' She ignores the pile of paperwork and jiggles the mouse, bringing the computer to life. 'In case you haven't noticed, the world's political leaders are descending on Rio for a weekend of speeches about global warming. Apparently it's a big deal, and the rest of the world, my man, is watching us.'

'Yeah? Sounds like they'll be making their own climate emergency, all the hot air they're going to be spouting.'

'That's funny, the protesters' slogan is 'Less Hot Air, More Action'. Snappy, huh?'

'I don't know, doesn't exactly roll off the tongue now, does it?' Jay frowns as he notices Quinn's feet on the desk. 'Why are you so interested?'

'Enrique is joining the protestors today.' Quinn logs onto the internet and calls up a news site. The shot of protesters, waving placards and blocking in the limousines, which was on the television, now fills the monitor's screen.

'Have you seen him yet?'

'Nah, not yet. Knowing Enrique, he probably isn't even out of bed.'

'Yeah, well, your boyfriend's probably got the right idea.'

Jay leaves her to watch the protesters on the computer and steps outside. As always, he turns and looks up at the sign over the door: 'J Stone Adventure Trips'. He puts his fingertips to his lips and kisses them, then reaches up and pats the sign. A good-luck gesture he performs every morning. Despite having run this business for the last three years, he still has trouble believing that people pay him to take them skydiving, caving, surfing, scuba-diving and mountain-trekking. He'd do it for free.

Next, he looks over the five sets of scuba-diving gear laid out in the pickup. Jay checks his watch, squinting in the harsh sunlight. He's got two sets of customers arriving in the next half hour. Jay is taking one group exploring Cueva Del Guácharo, a ten-kilometre cave system, whilst the other group is being taken scuba-diving off the local reefs where they will see, amongst other sea life, barracudas, turtles, rays and lobsters.

That is, if their diving instructor and guide turns up for work. Jay runs a hand through his long, sun-bleached hair. She's only worked for them for a few months, but she's been very reliable so far. Quiet, but efficient and good with the customers.

Pretty, too. Long legs, slim figure, wavy fair hair down over her shoulders, and the most amazing eyes. Just the kind of girl Jay likes. They get on great, as well. Sometimes he's sure he's caught her looking at him a certain way, but then whenever he's even got close to asking her out on a date, it seems like the shutters come down and she closes herself off from him. And those eyes . . . there's a sadness in them too, which he can't figure out.

Jay often thinks he should just forget about her and move on. After all, there are plenty of other women in Rio he could be asking out on a date. But somehow he just can't get her out of his head. It doesn't help that he's pretty sure she likes him too, but there is always that distance, that barrier she throws up between them.

Women! How is a man ever meant to understand them?

And right now this particular woman is late for work.

Jay pops his head back into the office. 'Hey, Quinn! Have you heard from Katrina? What's keeping her?'

# 2

Katrina blinks sweat out of her eyes, and promises herself that from now on she will only cross town on air-conditioned buses. Never mind the expense; the comfort will be worth it. Besides which, she always gets a seat on the more expensive buses. Standing on this bus amongst the press of hot, sweaty bodies, she is regretting her impulsive decision to try and economise this morning. Katrina thinks that maybe she will buy herself a bicycle soon, and start cycling into work.

The driver leans on his horn again, and swears at the crowd of protesters blocking his path. The bus has been stationary now for the last five minutes, and the driver has blasted his horn and sworn plenty, but no one is paying any attention.

Katrina looks at her watch. She's

already later than she would like, but still feels she can get to work in time to take her group out diving, if the bus starts moving soon.

The horn blares again and Katrina sees the driver lean out of his window and shout, '*Ô, meu! Que é isso?*'

It seems he has lost patience as he releases the handbrake and begins edging forward. Katrina cranes her neck to see better, as the protesters in front start shouting and banging their placards against the bus's bonnet. The driver slams on his brakes and, even though they were hardly moving, Katrina loses balance and bumps up against the man standing in front of her.

'Oh! I'm sorry, I mean, um, *perdão*.'

The old man turns and gazes at Katrina, a smile growing on his face. 'You speak English!'

'Yes, I do,' Katrina says, and finds herself smiling back. An elderly man, with a head full of white hair swept back from his forehead, he is impeccably dressed in a pale linen suit, although his shirt collar is open and he is not wearing a tie. The jacket seems far too big for him, as though he has lost a lot of weight very suddenly.

The old man clasps his hands together, as though in prayer. 'Oh, how wonderful. I've only been here two days, but I have missed someone to talk to in my own language.'

Katrina looks out of the bus windows, at the people milling around, some of them carrying placards, most just raising their fists as they chant something she does not understand. 'Well, looks like you've got your chance. I don't think we're going anywhere soon. What do you want to talk about?'

'I've always thought of that particular question as a guaranteed way to kill a conversation. When asked that, my mind invariably goes blank.'

Katrina laughs. 'You're right. Maybe we should start by introducing ourselves.' She holds out her hand. 'I'm Katrina.'

The old man takes her hand and

shakes it once. 'Pleased to meet you, Katrina. I'm Oliver. Now, when do you think these protesters will move out of the way, enabling us to resume our journey?'

'I've no idea; I just wish they would get a move on. What are they protesting about, anyway?'

'The lack of action on the part of the world's leaders regarding global warming, I believe. Don't you watch the news?'

'Not that often, recently. I don't have the time. My job keeps me pretty busy.'

'And what is your job that keeps you so busy?'

'I work in 'Adventure Tourism' — ' She holds up her hands and crooks her index and middle fingers as she says this. ' — giving mainly North American holiday-makers scuba-diving trips they hopefully will never forget.'

'I see. Sounds like fun.'

'Yeah, it's pretty good. And my boss is cool, too, which helps. He's Australian, and I'm sure he must be Crocodile

Dundee's cousin or something, he's so laid-back.' She thinks of Jay: tall, tanned, with an athletic body; his long, sun-bleached hair and surfer looks. With his easy charm and infectious smile, Katrina sometimes feels an electric attraction to him. And sometimes she thinks she sees it in his eyes too. But then the hurt and the sorrow come crushing back in, and she retreats back into herself, promising that she will never fall in love with anyone again. To do so would be a betrayal of Pete, something she could never do.

'And what other adventures do you provide?' the old man says.

'Caving, surfing, trips into the mountains, and . . . ' Sometimes she can hardly bring herself to say the words. ' . . . skydiving.'

'Oh dear, sounds far too adventurous for a man of my advanced years.' He pauses and glances out of the bus window, and for a moment Katrina thinks she sees an expression of fear passing over his features. 'Although I do seem to be in the middle of an adventure of my own making at the moment, whether I want one or not.'

'Sounds intriguing.' Katrina smiles. 'Are you a spy or something, like James Bond?'

The older man laughs. 'No, nothing anywhere near as exciting as that, my dear.'

The bus lurches forward again and Oliver stumbles, reaching out for a handhold. Katrina grabs his arm and helps steady him.

'Thank you. I'm not as steady on my feet as I once was. I would advise you to not grow old, as I have found little pleasure in it, but I am afraid I cannot suggest any worthy alternatives to ageing.'

'Are you sure you're all right?' Katrina says. She is having difficulty imagining why this old man should choose to come to Rio, even for an international conference. He seems lonely and bewildered, and Katrina gets the feeling he would be much better off at home in England.

‘Oh yes, I’m fine,’ he says, patting her hand. ‘Don’t you worry about me.’

The bus starts moving forward, and once more they are crawling through the chanting crowd of protesters.

* * *

Lowenstein feels a sudden need to unburden himself to this pretty young woman. The information he has been carrying with him for the last few days has become an intolerable burden. Especially here, in this raucous, hot city, where nobody speaks English, but everybody chatters away at him as though he understands what they are saying.

But, the scientist knows, to give Katrina the information he holds would be to place her in danger too. She can do nothing to help him; nobody can. Not yet, anyway. Not until he meets up with his old friend, Everett McCluskey. Until then, he simply has to keep moving and stay on the run, until the conference starts. And then he can present his information to the world, and everybody will know. Surely there would be no point in his enemies harming him then?

'May I ask what you are doing in Rio? Are you on holiday? You mentioned something about an adventure.'

Lowenstein flinches. He had not realised the girl was talking to him again. He looks around. The bus is still crawling through the crowds. He can see policemen pushing the protesters back, and clearing a path.

Lowenstein shakes his head. 'Sorry, my dear, I was miles away. No, I'm here for the conference. All very boring, I'm afraid.'

'Seems a lot of people are here for the conference. I'm guessing it's an important one.'

'The most important one of all,' Lowenstein says. 'Unless the world's leaders act together soon to combat climate change, we could find ourselves in an irreversible decline. The world's weather will become ever more unpredictable and damaging, and your children, I am afraid, will see some catastrophic changes across the globe in their lifetime.'

'That sounds terrible.' Katrina grabs a handrail as the bus lurches to a stop again and the driver begins shouting at the crowd once more. 'And you've come to Rio to present a talk at the conference?'

'I'm afraid not. I'm more of an uninvited guest.'

'That doesn't sound good. You make it sound as though they might turn you away.'

Lowenstein hesitates. 'There are certain people who would prefer if I did not attend, that is true.'

'I hope you don't get into any trouble.'

'Don't worry, I am meeting a friend here tomorrow — Everett McCluskey, an American politician. I am sure he will look after me.' Again Lowenstein feels the need to unburden himself. He decides to change the subject. 'Now tell me about yourself, as you seem to have avoided my rather obvious attempt at discovering more about you. Do you have children?'

'No, I'm single. No kids, no husband, just me.'

'I can't believe it. A pretty young woman like yourself, single?'

The old man suddenly senses that he has stepped over an invisible boundary, trespassed in some way. Katrina glances at the floor, and when she looks up at him he can see sadness etched into her features.

'I was engaged once, a couple of years ago. But he died.'

'I'm so very sorry.'

'We ran a skydiving school, and we were out with some students. We were teaching them synchronised freefall — you know, linking hands in a circle, that sort of thing. We got to the point where we all opened up our parachutes, but Pete just kept falling. It was a one-in-a-million event, a freak accident.

His main ’chute came out tangled, hardly opened at all; but when he opened his reserve, that one got tangled up in the other parachute which was flapping around just over his head.’

‘I’m so very sorry,’ Lowenstein says again. He can think of nothing else to say.

Katrina takes a deep breath. ‘I don’t know why I’m telling you all this, it’s the first time in ages I’ve spoken about it. After the funeral I didn’t know what to do with myself. I felt lost without Pete, broken. On impulse one day I decided to go travelling. I wound up in Rio about eight months ago, and I’ve been here ever since.’

‘And yet — forgive me for asking — you still go skydiving?’

Katrina shakes her head. ‘Oh no, no, never. I take the customers scuba-diving and I’m learning to surf too. But Jay — he’s my boss — he deals with the high altitude activities. He has no idea about any of this. Out here, in Rio, only my best friend Quinn knows about

Pete. And now you. Anyway, I've never even set foot on a plane in the last two years. I travelled by land and sea when I came out here.'

'Well, I think you are a very brave young woman,' Lowenstein says. These are the only words he can think of to comfort her.

Katrina glances around at the crowds still surrounding the bus. 'You know what? I've got no chance of getting to work on time now, but I can't bear to be on this bus any longer. I'm going to start walking.' She looks up at Lowenstein, and he can see she has been close to crying. 'It's been nice meeting you, Oliver. I hope the conference goes well for you, even if you are an uninvited guest.'

He inclines his head. 'Thank you. Please be careful, young lady. These crowds are beginning to look rowdy.'

Katrina flashes him a smile. 'Don't worry, I can take care of myself.'

*I do believe she can*, Lowenstein thinks as he watches her push her way down to the front of the bus. He continues watching her until she disappears into the crowd, and suddenly he feels old and weak, and incapable of the task ahead of him. *I should have told her. She could have helped me*.

The bus lurches into motion once more.

# 3

'Don't ever do that to me again, babes!' Quinn says. She has just returned from the bar, and hands a cocktail to Katrina. 'I thought I was gonna die down there.'

Katrina takes the brightly-coloured drink from her friend. Quinn has a habit of starting up a conversation as though they were already in the middle of it, and Katrina knows that, soon enough, she will find out what her friend is referring to.

It is the evening, and Katrina and Quinn are on one of their regular girls' nights out. Katrina sometimes wonders if Quinn would rather be spending more time with her boyfriend, Enrique. But Quinn is always the one to suggest the night out, and Katrina doesn't have many friends in Rio, and so she rarely turns the offer down.

Besides which, after arriving late at work this morning, she found Jay had taken his clients out diving. He had left a terse message for Katrina to do the admin work in the office, and now she is wondering how much longer she will be in her job. Tonight is a good opportunity to find out how mad Jay is.

They have a table in a booth, facing the empty dance floor of the Baronetti Bar and Club. The bar is futuristic, with neon strips glowing along its edges, and bottles of drinks on the rear wall lit up in a cold blue light.

The DJ is playing laid-back lounge music. It is early and quiet; still possible to have a conversation. Later, the music will be amped up with American anthems of hip-hop and Latin pop tunes, and the dance floor will fill with scantily-clad singles looking for a night of sex. A one-night stand is something Katrina has never chased after, and she has never been interested in clubbing, even as a teenager. She would prefer to drink elsewhere, but Rio seems to cater exclusively to young clubbers, and the Baronetti is better than most. At least at this time of the evening it is quiet and pleasant, and she can hold a conversation with Quinn.

By the time the music is turned up, and the dance floor filled with bodies, Katrina will be long gone. She will be back in her apartment, with her cat Atticus curled up on her lap, and her memories of Pete to keep her company.

'Was Jay very mad with me for turning up so late?'

'Katrina, babes, he'll never get angry with you.' Quinn sits down and throws back a revolting-looking drink, and slams the shot glass down on the table. Katrina sees a young guy looking over at them, but Quinn glowers at him and he quickly looks away.

'Are you sure? He didn't seem very happy with me when he got back from the diving trip. I tried explaining why I was late, but he just cut me off and told me not to do it again.'

'That's just his way. He's the man in

charge, right? It's his business, so he feels he has to strut his stuff sometimes, show everyone who the boss is. He don't mean anything by it. Besides which, I'm behind on the books and stuff, and he just knew you'd sort it out if he put you in the office, especially feeling bad about letting him down.'

Katrina's not so sure. Jay hadn't seemed happy with her earlier, not happy at all.

'Seriously, girl, you got nothing to worry about. If he really wanted to punish you for being late, he'd send you down that dark, stinky hole he calls a cave, like he did me today. You know, I'm the one who should be mad at you, because you're the reason I wound up going down there. If you'd arrived at work on time, you'd have been diving, Jay would have gone down the cave, and I would have been nice and happy and sitting in the office.'

'But you've been caving before, haven't you?'

'Yeah, but I don't never go down

Cueva Del Guácharo. I've been down there once before, and I vowed I ain't never going down there again. And there's a reason for that, hun.'

Katrina is glad to have Quinn as a friend. As she looks at her now, staring back at her, jaw jutting out, eyes wide, challenging Katrina to ask her what that reason is, she knows lesser mortals would wilt under her gaze, and flee into the evening. But Katrina loves Quinn dearly. She is the best friend she has ever had.

'So, Quinn, tell me, why do you never go down Cueva Del Guácharo?'

Quinn leans forward. 'Because of them damn oilbirds, that's why.'

Katrina smiles and takes a sip of her cocktail. There's a story coming here, she can tell. 'Okay, what are the oilbirds?'

'Went out with this guy few years ago, he's into caving. Man, he was so sexy, ever' time he climbed in bed with me, I thought I'd died and gone to heaven. So I'm thinking, I need to keep hold of this guy, not let no other girls get him. He's mine, see?'

Katrina nods, whilst Quinn takes a sip of her second cocktail.

'Well, I go down a few caves with him, and it's good, I'm having fun. We're an item now. I'm thinking this is the one for me, you know? Then he goes and says we should go down this cave system he's never taken me to before. Says it's got the most amazing caverns, cathedral-sized caverns full of 'tites and 'mites, the like you ain't ever seen before. Says if you never been there, you're not a caver.'

'Let me guess, this is Cueva Del Guácharo, right?'

'Damn right. Where the oilbirds live. And them things is nasty, dirty creatures. They're so ugly they only ever come out at night, 'cause they're too damn ashamed to be seen in daylight. And they're big, too.' She holds up her hands to indicate their size. 'But you know what the worst thing of all is?'

'Tell me, I'm dying to know.'

'They mess all over the cave floor,

that's what. And anybody who wants to go and explore these cathedral-sized caverns that everybody's so enamoured of, has got to crawl through all their guano. And it gets in your hair, on your face, over your hands, just everywhere.'

'And that's why you split up with your sexy boyfriend, because he dragged you through a cave full of guano?'

'Nah, I split with him because he was seeing some white girl on a foreign exchange programme, that's why.'

Katrina bursts out laughing, and hides her smile behind her hand. 'Oh, Quinn, I'm sorry, I didn't mean to laugh!'

'Yeah, well, don't be sorry, I'm not. He was a jerk, as it turned out.' Quinn scowls and leans across the table. 'Don't ever leave me to go down that stinking cave again, though. The stench was so powerful, I thought we was gonna suffocate.'

'Okay, I promise I'll do my best to keep you away from the Cueva Del Guácharo forevermore,' Katrina says solemnly.

'Well, ever' cloud has a silver lining,

right?' The ghost of a smile tilts the corners of Quinn's mouth up. 'When I got back home, I was so filthy I had to jump in the shower. Halfway through, Enrique decides maybe he could do with a wash, too. All turned out good in the end, know what I'm saying?'

Katrina holds her hands up. 'You don't have to tell me any more.' She picks up her handbag and pulls out her purse. 'Do you want another drink?'

In answer, Quinn thrusts her empty glass in the air and shouts, 'Caipirinha! Caipirinha!' and holds up two fingers. The bartender signals he has heard her and begins pouring their drinks.

'Look what some idiot did to my bag today,' Katrina says, holding up her bag and showing Quinn the ripped lining.

'How did that happen?'

'Oh, it was after I got off the bus. I was pushing my way through the crowds, all those protesters, and someone made a grab for my bag. We did a tug of war for a little while, and then I started screaming and shouting so he gave up and ran off, and disappeared into the crowd. But not before he managed to rip the lining.'

'You gonna get a new one?'

Katrina grimaces. 'On my salary? Are you kidding? No, I'll sew it up tonight when I get back.'

'Hey, girl, don't go home early. Why don't you hang around tonight? We'll dance and get drunk, yeah?'

Katrina looks down at the table. They go through this routine at least two or three times a week. 'I don't think so, Quinn. You know me, I'd prefer an early night.'

'Everyone likes an early night, hun, especially if it means sharing the bed with someone else.' Quinn takes Katrina's hand. 'Enrique'll be here later, and he's bringing his friend with him. And this guy, I gotta tell you, he's hot, baby, hot.'

Katrina takes her hand away, still not meeting Quinn's gaze. 'No, that's not a good idea, Quinn. You know why.'

Quinn reaches out and gently pushes Katrina's chin up until she is looking at her once again. 'Can't stay sad forever, babe.'

Katrina knows she's right, knows she's just doing what she thinks is best. But she's not ready yet. She can't face up to another relationship; it would be a betrayal of her love for Pete. In her heart she believes she will never be able to love anybody else in that way. She will never be ready. But she can't tell Quinn that.

'You're right,' she says. 'But not tonight, okay? I'm just . . . I'm just not ready.'

Their drinks arrive, the bartender placing them on the table. When he is gone, Quinn leans forward, fixing Katrina in her wide-eyed gaze. 'Listen, girl, I know you been through a rough time. But, in case you hadn't noticed, you're living in Rio de Janeiro now, and nobody's allowed to be sad in Rio. You so damn pretty, you know that? You got guys eyeing you up and down all the time, babe. You're hot property right now. You're so hot, I get the sweats just sitting next to you. So you can be sad a little bit longer, but you can't be sad forever. Know what I'm saying?'

'Will you stop it?' Katrina looks at Quinn, wondering how serious she is. 'I'm not hot property.'

'You so are!'

'So who are all these guys eyeing me up, and how come I've never seen any of them?'

Quinn sits back in her chair and laughs. 'Are you serious? Our glorious leader is totally crazy for you, for a start.'

'Jay? Now I know you're winding me up.'

'You're either blind or stupid, girl. Don't you see the way he looks at you every time you walk in the room?'

Katrina waves away the idea. 'Don't be silly. And don't look at me like that.' But what Quinn has said has pleased her, made her feel more positive about herself than she has in ages. She picks up her drink and downs it in one. 'I'm not getting drunk tonight, but let's have another, shall we?'

Quinn throws her head back and laughs. 'Way to go, girl! We gonna have some fun!'

# 4

At this moment in time, Professor Oliver Lowenstein is feeling every one of his seventy-six years. He pushes his way through the clubbers and revellers, not daring to look back to see if he has lost his pursuer. His right hand is pushed into his jacket pocket, gripping the USB stick he has carried everywhere with him for the last week. This metal tube of microchips has become like a talisman for him, but he suspects it will not bring him good fortune, but bad.

He can feel his heart thudding in his chest, like a racehorse's hooves beating against the ground. Sweat pours down his face, trickling down his torso and sticking his shirt to his flesh. The neon lights over the bars and clubs dazzle him, and he is pushed and pulled as he forces a path through the crowd.

Looking up, he briefly sees the statue

of Christ the Redeemer on Corcovado Hill. Bathed in red and blue lights, he is aglow against the purple of the night sky, his arms outstretched in a blessing as he towers over the city. Then Lowenstein turns a corner and he is stumbling down a cobbled side alley, the statue no longer visible. Long an atheist, he nevertheless offers up a swift prayer for protection, at least until the climate conference begins the day after tomorrow.

He knows now his chances of staying alive are slim. Earlier, when the bus finally let him off at his hotel, he saw the suntanned man sitting in the hotel lobby, waiting. Lowenstein froze, suddenly helpless with indecision. His instincts told him to run, but he had nowhere to flee to in this unfamiliar city. As he stood there, his mind locked in uncertainty, the shaven-headed man looked up and their eyes met. The man began to rise from his seat, but the old man turned and pushed his way back outside.

He has been running all day, and now he is exhausted. All he can do is try to disappear amongst the young people partying on the streets.

He walks up a flight of stone steps, the edges worn smooth over decades of use. Ancient buildings tower over him on either side, hemming him in, until he is out the other side. The deep, percussive bass of modern music, alien to his ears, pounds out of a bar across the street. Its neon sign, seeming to pulse in time with the music, proclaims itself to be the Baronetti Bar and Club. Men and women are laughing and screaming, chattering and singing, as they push past him.

Lowenstein is lost, and feels helpless. It has been many years since he last cried, when his beloved Margaret died, leaving him alone after 41 years of marriage. But now he wants to cry again, weep with frustration and anger. He is so close to delivering his world-changing information to the World Climate Conference, and yet the barriers between him and his goal now seem insurmountable.

The bar across the crowded street suddenly seems his only hope. It will be dark inside, he thinks, and he may be able to find a quiet, hidden corner in which to sit out most of the night. He has no idea when the clubs and bars close, but he is sure it will not be until the early hours of the morning. Then he will be one day closer to the conference, and he can plan his next moves.

He steps forward, when a man walks in front of him, blocking his path. He places his hands on Lowenstein's chest and pushes him back into the alley. The old man totters at the top of the flight of steps, and he feels the pull of gravity, ready to send him in a bone-breaking plunge down to the bottom. But powerful hands grip him by the shoulders and he is guided to the side, against a wall.

'Professor Lowenstein, how nice to meet you at last,' the man says. He has an American accent and he is movie-star handsome, short dark hair parted neatly to the left, sunglasses propped over his forehead. He is wearing a light jacket over a T-shirt, and white slacks.

'Who are you?'

'Ben Stahl, CIA. We've been keeping an eye on you ever since you got here.' The man looks down the flight of steps and then back at the clubbers. 'I wanted to keep a low profile, but you look like you need help right now.'

Lowenstein nods, relief flooding his system. His legs suddenly go weak and he fears he might crumple to the floor. 'I'm being followed.'

Stahl nods. 'Yeah, we know. An Iranian hitman, goes by the name of Kubaschi. You're a lucky man, Professor. Kubaschi has a notoriously successful hit rate. And a most unpleasant modus operandi.'

'What do you mean?'

Stahl glances around again. Lowenstein notices beads of sweat on his forehead. 'Well, now's probably not the best time to talk about this, but let's just say he takes a lot of pleasure in his job, and that some of his victims have been known to suffer a long and painful death.'

'Oh, dear Lord,' Lowenstein whispers. He wanted none of this. He is a mild-mannered, retired scientist, who should be sitting in his cottage in Porthleven, sipping whisky and reading *The Times*.

'But not to worry,' Stahl says, flashing him a big Hollywood smile. 'You're safe now. Just one thing, Professor: do you have the information on you, or have you put it somewhere safe?'

The sense of safety and security that had enveloped Lowenstein suddenly begins to slip away. The old man feels his bladder loosen slightly as he wonders why the CIA would be interested in a case of industrial espionage, originating in Europe.

Slowly he releases his grip on the USB stick and withdraws his hand from his pocket. He wipes his damp palm on his trousers.

'No, it's somewhere safe. I couldn't chance carrying it with me.' He wills himself to stop talking, afraid of giving something away.

'Very prudent of you, Professor Lowenstein. But you're safe now. Perhaps if we could go and collect it, and then I can lead you to our safe house.'

Lowenstein sees the American's eyes narrow as he regards him, and he realises his face has betrayed him, that his fear and suspicion of this man are clear to be seen in his lined features.

Just then a firecracker explodes in the street. Stahl whirls round, and the old man sees him reaching into his jacket and half pulling out a black, shiny pistol. Realising his mistake, he slides the gun back, but Lowenstein has seen his opportunity.

With all the might he can muster from his old, frail body, he shoves Stahl and starts running. Diving headlong into the crowd, Lowenstein glances back and sees that the American has stumbled and fallen on his backside. But he is already clambering to his feet, his hand slipping under his jacket again, his eyes fixed on the scientist.

Pushing and elbowing his way through the crowd, Lowenstein struggles to see where he is going. His vision is blurred, and his heart is thumping painfully in his chest. He stumbles through the revellers and finds himself at the back of a queue, waiting to enter a door, guarded by a bouncer. The music is so loud he can hardly bear it, and the neon sign he saw earlier towers over him.

He pushes forward again, gripping the USB stick tight in his fist.

# 5

'What?' Katrina can hardly hear Quinn; she can just see her mouth moving in the strobe lights from the dance floor. She knows she should have gone home an hour ago, before the clubbers arrived, before the music was amped up to ear-shredding levels.

Before she had too many cocktails, and got so drunk.

'I said,' Quinn yells, leaning forward, her face inches from Katrina's ear, 'Enrique will be here any moment. You should stay a bit longer.'

'What, and meet this hot guy you keep telling me about?' Katrina picks up her bag, slipping the strap over her shoulder, deciding that now is the right time to leave.

But when Katrina looks up, she is suddenly fascinated to see that her friend looks embarrassed. Quinn opens her mouth to say something, but then stares over Katrina's shoulder at a disturbance behind her.

Katrina turns and looks, and then stands up as she sees the old man stumbling through the club. He has one hand in his jacket pocket, and the other clutches his chest. He looks confused and in pain, and then Katrina realises that she knows him. Behind him a huge, broad-shouldered bouncer has snagged the back of the old man's jacket.

'Oliver!'

Lowenstein sees Katrina, as he slips out of the oversized jacket and stumbles towards her. The slow-witted bouncer is left standing motionless in momentary confusion, holding an empty jacket where only a moment ago he had a person.

Katrina grabs him as he falls against her. He hardly weighs anything, slumped in her arms. He looks up at her, grimacing with pain. His mouth opens, his lips struggling to form words that Katrina cannot hear over the thumping bass of the music. She inclines her head, can feel his hot breath on her ear, and then he is being lifted off her, taken from her. She wants to stop them, to shout at them to leave him alone. She is worried for the old man, scared that they might take him to the big, burly bouncer, who will then throw him out of the club.

Lowenstein is carried to a table and laid out, and Katrina realises that people are trying to help him. But when she sees his eyes rolling upwards, and his face contorted in agony, a cold dread settles in her stomach.

*He's dying*, she thinks, and for a moment she is falling through space, powerless to act as she watches Pete plummet to his death once more. *Will this never end?* she thinks. *Am I always destined to be trapped on the sidelines, watching people die around me? Who will it be next? Quinn? Jay?*

'What's happening?' Quinn is standing beside her, snapping her out of her thoughts. 'Do you know him?'

'Not really. I met him earlier today, on the bus. We . . . we talked.'

Someone turns off the music, and the relative silence is shocking. Oliver Lowenstein is surrounded by people now, and Katrina can no longer see him.

'Someone get a doctor!' a voice shouts. 'He's having a heart attack!'

Katrina stifles a cry. She hardly knew this man, met him only once, but she feels so desperately sorry for him. Quinn places an arm around her shoulder. This only serves to heighten her emotions, and before she knows it she is crying.

Katrina is dabbing at her eyes when Enrique arrives, with Jay trailing behind him. Enrique is tall and muscular, and his dark skin glistens under the club's lights. Almost always smiling, now he looks sombre and worried as he gazes at Katrina. 'What's happened here?'

'Some old dude that Katrina met earlier just collapsed on her,' Quinn says.

Jay takes Katrina's hand. 'Come on, why don't you sit down for a moment?' He glances over at the crowd still surrounding the old man. 'How did you know him?'

Katrina shakes her head and takes more tissues from her handbag. 'I didn't know him, not really. I just met him on the bus earlier today, when we were stuck in the crowd. He's a nice old man.'

'I wonder what he's doing out here, at this time of night?'

'He said he was here for the World Climate Conference,' Katrina says, dabbing at her eyes again. She is feeling a little more in control of herself, and wonders if the tears were truly for the old man, or if she was simply reliving her grief over Pete.

'Poor guy. I hope he's okay.'

Flashing blue lights through the open door signal the arrival of an ambulance. The crowd parts for the paramedics as they run inside, clutching their medical bags. Two of the young clubbers who helped carry Lowenstein onto the table walk past, and Katrina hears one say to the other, '*Eles são demasiado tarde, ele está morto*.'

Her Portuguese is still not very good.

She looks at Quinn. 'What did he say?'

Quinn shakes her head, looking miserable.

'Tell me. What did he say?'

'He said, 'They are too late, the old man is dead'.'

Katrina bows her head, as tears fall from her eyes.

* * *

The night sky is clear, the stars shining brighter than Katrina would have thought possible before she came to Rio. Everything seems brighter here, more vivid somehow, than anywhere else she has lived.

'I suppose you think I'm a silly little girl, crying over somebody I never knew, don't you?' Katrina says, as they walk side-by-side in the early hours of the morning.

Jay takes her by the hand and stops her, turning her to face him. 'Of course I don't. Most people don't seem to care much about anything or anyone these days, unless it involves themselves. I think it's beautiful that you mourned for him, even though you hardly knew him.'

'Thank you, that's a lovely thing to say.'

They start walking again, the cool night air refreshing after the closeness of the club. Katrina had been reluctant to go straight home; she hadn't wanted to be on her own. Quinn suggested they go somewhere for coffee, and the four of them had sat at a table outside a late-opening coffee bar, talking into the early hours.

Finally the two couples had parted ways, and Katrina had meant to go home. But since then Jay and Katrina have been wandering the cobbled streets of Santa Teresa. The old, colonial buildings, now turned into art galleries and restaurants that line the quaint, winding alleyways, have had a calming effect on the young woman. She feels sad, but much more at peace.

'I thought the police were never going

to let us go,' Jay says. 'They seemed particularly interested in talking to you, especially the boss guy. What was his name?'

'Detective Inspector Benzali. Although he said I could call him Antonio. He was nice.'

'Yeah, well, you need to watch out for the nice ones. They've always got something up their sleeve, you know, like an ulterior motive or something.'

'Does that include you?' Katrina regrets saying it as soon as the words have left her mouth. She sounds like she is flirting, but that wasn't her intention.

Jay stops and leans on a low wall, looking out over the twinkling orange lights of the city below them, and the darkness of the sea beyond. His long hair flops over his eyes and he brushes it back. 'Nah, what you see is what you get with me, mate.'

Katrina joins him by the wall. 'I wonder what Oliver was running from. He seemed scared, desperate. Do you think he came to the Baronetti because he knew I was there?'

'Seems unlikely. How on earth would he have known where you were?'

Katrina looks at Jay, and a thought occurs to her. 'Hey, what were you doing there, anyway?'

'I came with Enrique.'

'So what happened to the hot guy that Quinn told me Enrique was bringing along?' She stops, and feels herself colouring up in embarrassment. 'Oh, that was you, wasn't it? Quinn and Enrique were trying to match-make us. No wonder Quinn looked so embarrassed just before you arrived.'

'I had no idea what was going on,' Jay says. 'As far as I knew, me and Enrique were just going out for a drink. But then we got to the Baronetti, and I saw you and Quinn.'

'I can't believe they would do that. Quinn knows how I feel about . . . '

Jay turns and looks at her. 'About what?'

Katrina sighs. 'Oh, nothing.'

Jay looks at her for a few moments

longer, and Katrina wonders if he is going to ask her again. She feels she could tell him right at this moment. Maybe it's the sound of the waves on the beach below, maybe the canopy of stars overhead, and the smell of jasmine on the cool night breeze. Maybe it's because it's just the two of them, and they've been talking alone for the last few hours, and a sense of intimacy has grown between them. Whatever the reason, Katrina suddenly feels she could tell Jay all about Pete, about what happened. No, more than that, she *wants* to tell him. If he will just ask her again, she knows she will tell him everything.

But Jay turns and looks out at the ocean again, and the feeling passes, and the shutters come back down, and she knows she can never tell him.

'Well, that's Quinn and Enrique for you,' Jay says. 'They've been trying to pair me off with a woman for the last year or two.'

'What? Who with?' Is that a pang of jealousy she feels? She tells herself not to be silly. Jay means nothing to her.

'Oh, anyone, really. They seem to think it's time I settled down, stop acting like a big kid in a toyshop, and get serious for once.'

Katrina's mind is whirling. What does he mean, get serious? She suddenly realises she has no idea of the kind of person Jay really is. For all she knows he could have a different woman every night. Is that what he means by acting like a big kid in a toyshop? There are so many beautiful women in Rio, far prettier and more confident than Katrina. Jay could have any woman he wants.

But then why does that bother her? She isn't interested in Jay. Is she?

'So . . . are you seeing anyone at the moment?'

Jay continues looking out to sea. 'Nah. I think I'm going to give women a rest for a while. It's fun to begin with, but then it all starts getting so complicated. They want me to think about settling down, moving in with me. And, worst of all, they all want me to start being more careful, you know?'

'What do you mean?'

'My job. I've never met a girl yet who was happy about me leaping out of an airplane. Every time I do it, they all seem convinced I'm going to die. It's ridiculous, really. You'd think I'd be able to meet a girl who shared my interests, or at least understood me a little better. But no, they all turn out to be airheads, just want to party, party, party.'

*I understand you*, Katrina thinks. *I know what drives you to do the things you do. But I can understand their fears for your safety, too. I understand that far too well.*

'So, what about you? I guess you're not seeing anybody if Quinn's trying to pair you up with somebody?' Jay is still looking out to sea, avoiding eye contact. Suddenly it occurs to Katrina that he is possibly a little nervous, slightly unsure of himself. This is not the Jay she has grown to know, who always seems so self-confident. Is he asking her this question for a reason? If she says she is single, what will he say next? Is Quinn right? Does Jay like her?

Again, Katrina wonders if she should tell Jay about Pete, about his skydiving accident. But she is scared, more frightened with her feet on the ground than she has ever been up in the air, waiting to make that leap into the atmosphere.

'Well, don't worry about it,' Jay says, and Katrina realises she has stalled too long, and the moment has passed. 'You can tell me another time.'

Forgetting who she is with, Katrina thumps the top of the wall in frustration, allowing her anger with herself get the better of her.

'You okay?' Jay says.

'Um, yeah. Just thinking about Quinn and Enrique, setting us up like that. I'm going to kill Quinn when I see her tomorrow.'

'It already is tomorrow, look.' Jay points out to the horizon, at the first glow of the approaching dawn.

Katrina sighs, and folds her arms around herself. 'What a night. I'm usually in bed by eleven.'

Jay laughs. 'I hope you're not going to be late for work again today. We've got a group of nine Chilean rugby players booked in for a dive. They want to explore the Ilha Grande coral reef.'

'Nine rugby players! You're kidding me, right?'

'No, I'm serious.' Jay laughs again. 'Don't worry, I'm coming down with you. Nine is too big a group to guide all by yourself. Besides, they want to explore the wreck of the *Cavo Artemidi*. No way you can do that by yourself.'

'Okay, good. Hey, this will be only our second dive together.'

'Yeah, that's right. And the first one doesn't count, to be honest. That was more of a job interview. Tell you what, I was desperate for a dive partner for the business, so I was ready to take you on unless you were an absolute disaster underwater. But you blew me away with how good you are.'

'Thank you,' Katrina says. She feels almost ridiculously pleased by the compliment.

'No, I mean it. Thing is, I think we should start expanding your role in the business soon. You know, we should get you underground; that way you can start leading some caving expeditions too.'

'As long as I don't have to go down Cueva Del Guácharo. Quinn's told me all about the oilbirds.'

Jay laughs again. 'Quinn and her oilbirds. She loves it really. The other thing we need to get you trained up in is the skydiving. I bet you'll have a natural talent for that.'

'Oh no, I don't think so. I'm not very good with heights, to be honest.' Katrina, feeling she is on uncomfortable ground, decides to change the subject. 'Is Jay your proper name, or is it short for something, like James, or Jason?'

'Everyone calls me Jay, but that's not my name, it's my initial. You know, like it says over the door, J Stone.'

'So, what's your name?'

Jay smiles and shakes his head. 'Nah, I can't tell you that, not yet anyway. You'll just laugh.'

'I won't laugh, I promise.'

'That's what everybody says. And then they fall over, they're laughing so hard.'

'Okay.' Katrina thinks for a moment. 'Let me see, it's got to be something unusual then, like maybe . . . Jedediah!'

'Nope.' He shakes his head, grinning.

'Was I close?'

'Nowhere near. You're so cold, you're subzero at the moment.'

'Johnson? Jeremiah? Jasper? Jackie?'

'You'll never get it. Not in a million years'

'Come on, it can't be that bad.' She leans into him, nudging him slightly.

'Uh uh, no way.' He looks out to sea, at the brightening horizon, declaring the subject closed.

'Okay, I get the hint.' Katrina leans her elbows on the wall and looks out to sea too. The silence between them is companionable, comfortable. The tension she felt earlier has dissipated now, and the young woman feels happier than she has felt in a long time.

She glances at Jay, trying not to make it obvious. He is still gazing out to the horizon, and seems not to notice her looking at him. Katrina is surprised that part of her is wishing the night would not end. She has enjoyed walking the streets, talking about stuff, some of it serious, some of it not.

And it's hard not to notice, but he's an attractive guy, too, with his surfer hair and tanned body. Jay has an easy smile that can lighten Katrina's mood in a moment. Just the opposite of Pete, who could often be very solemn and serious.

Katrina bites her lip and looks away. Suddenly she feels as though she has stabbed herself through the heart, and sullied her fiancé's memory. How could she compare any other man with her only true love? Her feelings of happiness quickly dissolve, leaving her with an empty ache and a sadness.

'Let's get back,' she says, and begins walking down the street.

* * *

Ben Stahl watches the couple walking away. He has been trailing them ever since they left the Baronetti. Now he is tired and irritable.

He is absolutely positive that the old man gave something to the young woman when he collapsed against her in the bar. Stahl knows Lowenstein was lying when he claimed the information he needed was in safekeeping. He could see it in his eyes, in his posture. Thinking back on that moment, Stahl is convinced he had what he needed in his jacket pocket. Probably on an encrypted USB stick.

The old man had surprised him, pushing him out of the way like that. Just a lucky shove on his part, catching Stahl off balance. The American had been tempted to shoot him there and then, and even went so far as to get his gun out. Not a good idea, though. Not with all those people around — too many witnesses, too difficult to get away quickly.

So he followed him into the bar, knowing the old man couldn't get far. Then it all went badly wrong when he collapsed. The American still thought he had a chance, though. He got in amongst the crowd surrounding the scientist on the table and, under the pretext of checking his vital signs, Stahl had performed a perfunctory search of his pockets.

Nothing.

The girl. She has to have what he wants. What he has been sent halfway around the world to get. They told him to do it quietly, not to leave a mess behind. With the exception of Lowenstein, they want no dead bodies. No corpses, no questions, no investigation by the police. They need to be seen to be completely aboveboard on this, not involved in any suspicious activity at all.

The old-timer has done them all a

big favour, in some ways. Dropping dead of a heart attack like that was very considerate of him, no questions to ask there. But still, Stahl needs to find the USB stick. But how to do that without leaving a mess?

That puts Stahl in a difficult position. Normally he would have just murdered the couple and then searched the girl's body until he found what he wanted. But no. This time he is going to have to be a little bit more subtle.

The first objective, then, is to discover where she lives. Once that is accomplished, he is sure he will soon find what he needs. And if he doesn't . . . well, perhaps he will just have to make a mess after all. His employers will not be too angry once they realise he has what they need.

Stahl steps out of the shadows and follows the couple as they walk down the cobbled street, back into the city.

# 6

'Hey! Get off there, mister! What do you think you're up to?'

The cat jumps off the kitchen counter and slinks between Katrina's ankles, purring. Katrina squats and tickles him between his ears. 'Anybody would think I didn't feed you.'

Atticus looks up at her with his big, round eyes, and his purr grows in intensity.

'No way, mister. You've had your breakfast, and that's my lunch you were eyeing up. If I feed you any more often you're gonna get fat. Then where would you be, huh? What use do I have for a big old cat who's too fat to run and jump and catch mice?'

In reply, Atticus rubs his head against her ankles and then stalks off with his tail in the air.

Katrina looks at her handbag, examining her sewing job. Her mother is the professional seamstress in the family, and Katrina has picked up her skills. She's pleased with the job she has done, and doubts anybody else would notice it had been ripped. It's a good job, too — she can't afford a new handbag, not unless she gets a pay rise with the new duties Jay is talking about giving her.

Katrina's attention is grabbed by the television, as she hears mention of the Rio 2016 World Climate Conference. *That was what Oliver Lowenstein was attending. But what did he say? Something about being an uninvited guest?*

A middle-aged man, looking cool and collected in his suit, despite the heat, is being interviewed in a large lobby busy with people in the background. 'Rio 2016 may be our last chance for the countries of the world to come together and work towards averting irreversible climate change.' His name scrolls across the bottom: Everett McCluskey, US Under Secretary of State for the Environment.

'But what do you say to those who

charge you with being too lenient on the oil companies, in particular their lack of environmental responsibility?' the interviewer says. 'Some campaigners go so far as to claim your position as Under Secretary of State for the Environment is compromised by alleged business interests in the oil industry.'

McCluskey gives the interviewer a tired smile, as though he has heard all of this before. 'My business interests have already been published and made widely available, as per the rules of government. And if you don't already know my stance on the environment, then it will become blindingly clear over the course of the conference.' At that point, the picture cuts back to the studio.

Yawning, Katrina switches off the television and puts on a pot of coffee to brew. McCluskey — wasn't that the name of the politician that Oliver Lowenstein mentioned? She wonders if the American knows about his friend yet.

Katrina yawns again. She's not sure how safe it is to be taking a group of customers diving, having had no sleep for twenty-four hours. But Jay's the boss, and he seemed none the worse for wear for a lack of sleep when they parted an hour ago, although he did seem a little subdued.

'Only got yoursel' to blame for that, hun,' she says, imitating Quinn's sassy, no-nonsense voice.

Privately, she has already forgiven her friend for attempting to match-make the two of them, although she's not going to tell her that just yet. She knows she only had the best intentions, and it did lead to a pleasant couple of hours strolling through the streets of Santa Teresa with Jay.

Katrina feels bad that the night ended as it did. She hadn't meant to give Jay the cold shoulder, and she is sure he was utterly mystified at her sudden change in mood. But her loyalty to, and feelings for, Pete are still way too strong to be easily put aside. There are days when she wonders if, besides the ever-present grief over his death, she sometimes feels guilty too.

Guilty that he died while she lived. Guilty that maybe she could have done something to save him. She has mulled over his accident many times in the last two years, and can think of nothing that she could have done to rescue him. But still, she carries a subtle sense of blame with her through the day, and in the night the feeling of guilt haunts her dreams.

Sometimes, in her darker moments, she thinks that if not for Quinn, Rio de Janeiro may have been her last stop anywhere.

Quinn has been her rock since she arrived in Rio. Still raw with grief, despite having travelled halfway around the world to escape her ghosts, Katrina had turned up in Rio with barely any money left, and no ticket to go home. Even if she had had a ticket, she's not sure she would have gone back. To return to her home town, to live with her parents again, and be surrounded by well-meaning, sympathetic family and friends? No, that would have been a torture she could not have endured. At least on her travels, making her way through North Africa, and then North and finally South America, she only carried her own emotional baggage. To live with others who knew him, to be reminded of him every day by the sympathetic glances, the kindnesses — it all would have been too much.

Katrina is certain she would have gone insane with grief.

So she arrived in Rio, her number-one priority to find a place to live and a job to pay the rent. The only vacancies available in the city of Rio de Janeiro seemed to be bar work, so that's what she did. After all, how hard could it be, serving drinks?

Her first evening on the job started well. The bar was quiet, and she was able to successfully interpret the requests for most drinks. But then the rush started, the music was turned up, and Katrina began to panic. Beneath the deep pounding bass of the DJ's tunes, the customers' requests became unintelligible, and in the strobing lights of the bar, the bottles of alcohol all looked the same.

When she dropped the full bottle of bourbon, shards of glass and whisky spraying across the floor, she burst into tears. The customers cheered and the manager began yelling at her. Never one to stand by while someone needs help, Quinn had come to her rescue. She pulled her outside, calmed her down, and listened whilst Katrina unloaded her grief, and told Quinn everything in a torrent of tears. The following morning, Quinn arranged a job interview with *J Stone Adventure Trips*, and a new phase in Katrina's life started.

Eight months later, and Katrina recognises that she has at least found a measure of peace and acceptance being here. She has no idea how long she will stay in Rio, but she is certain that wherever she goes and whatever she does from now on, she can never return home.

Katrina snaps the lid closed on her lunch, a chicken salad, and is pouring herself a strong black coffee, when her doorbell rings.

* * *

Stahl watches from his concealed entrance as the cop enters the apartment block. He has to assume that he is on his way to see the woman, and so he resigns himself to a longer wait than he anticipated.

He just hopes the two young thugs he has already given money to, with the promise of more later, will have the sense to hang around and wait, too. That is if the sight of the cop hasn't already scared them off. He wonders if he should go and check on them, but decides against it. Their jaws dropped when he told them how much he was willing to pay for their involvement.

'Just rough her up a little bit if you have to,' he told them. 'But the main thing is to get her handbag. Or if she's not carrying a handbag, anything else that she has on her. Just steal something.'

The plan is then for Stahl to come rushing in, her knight in shining armour. He told them he will have to make it look authentic; he's going to have to rough them up a little bit. They might end up with a few bruises, maybe some minor abrasions, nothing too much. They were happy with that, too busy thinking how much they could score with the money he was going to pay them.

No, he decides against going to check on them. They aren't going to miss out on a big payday like today just because they saw a cop.

Stahl takes a couple of uppers, swallowing the pills dry. He has to stay alert, on top of his game. If he can get the USB stick today, he can be back in New York by tomorrow. He can arrange transfer of the USB stick, and the information it holds, and then he can collect his cash.

The thought of his money makes him smile. The amount they are paying him, he might even be able to retire soon.

# 7

'Would you like coffee? I've just brewed some,' Katrina says.

'Thank you, that would be nice,' Detective Inspector Benzali replies. He takes the mug of coffee and sits down at the small kitchen table. Atticus entwines himself around the visitor's ankles, sniffing at the hem of his trousers, his tail whipping from side to side.

'Ah, you can smell the dog, can you not?' Benzali bends down and strokes the cat, who responds by rolling over and exposing his tummy.

'You big softy, Atticus,' Katrina says, sitting down opposite the policeman.

'He is saying he trusts me, he is my friend. Despite the fact that I smell of dog.'

'Perhaps he is a good judge of character.'

Benzali smiles and straightens up,

leaving Atticus lying on his back, his legs splayed in the air. The policeman is a middle-aged man, with a gentle smile and sad-looking eyes. Katrina has already warmed to him, and feels she can tell him anything.

'I am sorry to bother you so early this morning, but a policeman is never really off duty, and as I had a few more questions to ask you, and I was already in the area . . . ' He smiles apologetically, and shrugs his shoulders.

'That's all right. I'm happy to answer any questions you have.' Katrina glances at the clock. 'But I'm afraid I do have to leave for work soon.'

'Then I will be as quick as I can, and let you get on your way.' He pulls a notebook from his pocket and flips it open. 'This poor man, Professor Oliver Lowenstein. You say you have never met him before?'

'Oh, I have met him. I met him yesterday morning, on the bus.'

Benzali consults his notebook. 'But last night you said you did not know him.'

'Well, that's true, I don't — I mean didn't, know him. I only met him once, and we had a brief conversation before I got off the bus. The next time I saw him was in the club.'

The detective mulls this over for a few moments. 'On the bus, what did you talk about?'

'Oh, I don't know. Just the usual kind of things strangers might say, I suppose. I asked him if he was on holiday, but he said no, he was going to the climate conference.'

'Was he a delegate there? Was he speaking?'

'No.' Katrina thinks for a moment. 'He said something a little odd, actually. He said he was an uninvited guest.'

'How so?'

'Um, I don't know. To be honest, he learned far more about me than I did about him. He was a lovely old man, easy to talk to. He did seem very passionate about the conference's aims, though, to prevent climate change getting worse. Oh, and he said he was a friend of one of the United States politicians who is here, too. I saw him on the news this morning.'

'Can you remember his name?'

'Hmm, I'm not sure.' Katrina frowns, trying to recall the name she heard just a few minutes ago. 'It kind of sounded a little bit Scottish, I think. You know, Mac something or other. Oh, that's it, Everett McCluskey!'

Benzali makes a note of the name in his book. 'Did he ask anything of you? A favour of some sort?'

Katrina shakes her head. 'No, I'm sure I would have remembered if he had.'

'And he didn't arrange to meet you at the Baronetti later that night?'

'No, definitely not. It was a big surprise to me when he staggered through the door.'

Atticus surprises them both by leaping up onto Katrina's lap, making her jump. She gives the cat a stern look and then forgives him by stroking him.

'Professor Lowenstein was still alive

when he got to the hospital,' Benzali says softly.

Katrina looks up at him, shocked. 'But, I thought he had died at the club.'

'He was hovering between life and death, and he died later, in the early hours of the morning. But before he died he roused slightly, and regained consciousness. I was there, and he pulled me close, and he whispered your name, Katrina. Three times he whispered your name.'

Katrina looks at the detective, wide-eyed. She is thinking of her and Jay walking the streets of Santa Teresa, laughing and joking, and looking at the stars and the ocean, whilst Lowenstein fought for his life in the hospital. And then she is thinking of the moment in the club, when Lowenstein fell into her arms. His lips were moving, soundlessly beneath the loud music, and Katrina had felt he was trying to tell her something. She had inclined her head to hear better, but then he was being pulled off her, carried to the table where he was laid out.

'I don't understand,' she whispers.

'No, neither do I.' Benzali sighs. 'And it gets more mysterious. We found his passport and did some checks. It seems your kindly old professor is a wanted man.'

'No, he can't be.'

'From what I have gathered he has been working part-time on a top-secret project for Coeus Petroleum. But then, just over a week ago, he disappeared — with details of an important new development that the oil company has been working on. Professor Lowenstein had a warrant out for his arrest, I'm afraid, on charges of industrial espionage.'

Katrina thinks of the kindly old man she met on the bus, asking her about family, about children, sympathising with her over her loss. She finds it hard to believe this same man could be a criminal.

'Lowenstein did mention one more name besides yours before he died,' Benzali says.

Katrina encircles Atticus in her arms, and pulls him a little closer. She feels Benzali is about to tell her something she does not want to hear. 'What name did he mention?'

'Have you heard of a man by the name of Kubaschi?'

'No, never. Who is he, do you know?'

'Kubaschi is an Iranian contract killer.'

Katrina's hand flies to her mouth, and Atticus jumps from her lap, startled by the movement. 'Oh my . . . Oh no.'

'I am sorry to worry you so, but if Kubaschi is involved in this affair then we have a very serious problem. I wanted to let you know, but I am sorry to cause you anxiety. Our one ray of hope is this: Kubaschi was reported killed late last year. The killing was witnessed, the body was identified, and it seemed an open and shut case. I read the news myself, and breathed a sigh of relief that this contemptible human being was no longer with us.'

'But now you think . . . ?'

Benzali shrugs. 'I don't know what to think. At the moment I can only deal with what I know, and I know very little. Professor Lowenstein spoke Kubaschi's name in his dying moments. What that means, I cannot say.'

'What do you think I should do?'

Benzali lifts his mug to his mouth and drains the last of his coffee. He seems to Katrina to be taking his time, and she wonders if he is stalling while he thinks of an answer.

Finally he replaces the now empty mug on the table. 'That was very nice coffee, just how I like it. Thank you. Now, as to what you should do, you should live your life as normal. What other option can I offer you? Perhaps I could advise you to take the next flight home, but then I see you are building yourself a life out here, and so why would you want to go home? No, you should carry on with your normal routine. You should go to work, go out with your friends, come home, do whatever you do with your life.'

'But . . . '

'But nothing. I can offer you no police protection as no threat has been made against your life. I can offer you a description of Kubaschi, that you may look out for him, but the description would be useless. Why? Because the description is this: Kubaschi was a man of medium height and medium weight, with no distinguishing features about him. And besides which, he was a master of disguise, as his profession required him to be.'

'I see your point.' Katrina glances at the clock on the wall, and takes a deep breath, trying to dispel the butterflies in her stomach. 'Well, as you suggest that I stick to my normal routine, I shall say I'm sorry, but I have to be going soon, or I'll be late for work. I was late yesterday and I don't want it to happen again today.'

Benzali stands up and slides his chair under the table. 'My apologies for keeping you so long, and for causing you unnecessary anxiety. You have been very kind to sit here and answer my questions, and give me coffee.'

'I'm sorry I couldn't be of more help.'

Benzali produces a business card from his pocket and passes it to Katrina. 'Here you will find my office number and my mobile. If you think of any further information, no matter how useless you might think it, or if you have any reason whatsoever to be concerned for your safety, then please do not hesitate to contact me. Any time of day or night I will answer your call, and myself or one of my colleagues can be here within ten minutes.'

'Thank you.' Katrina takes the card and stands up too.

The detective walks to the door, replacing his notebook in his pocket. As he opens the door he turns and says, 'Goodbye, Katrina, have a nice day. As I said, please do not hesitate to call, whatever the reason.'

'I won't.' Katrina smiles. 'I'll be in touch straight away.'

Once the detective has gone, Katrina rushes around her apartment, checking all the windows are shut, apart from one which she leaves locked partially open for Atticus to squeeze in and out of. She puts her lunch in her rucksack, replaces the items she removed from her handbag and puts that in her rucksack too. She does her best to put Lowenstein, and the hitman Kubaschi, out of her mind. Benzali is right — what can she do, other than carry on with her daily routine?

She halts at the door when Atticus gives her a plaintive, drawn-out meow. He is sitting by his food bowl, gazing at Katrina with big, round eyes.

Katrina throws her hands in the air. 'Okay, you win! I give up!'

She opens a kitchen cupboard and pulls out a bag of cat food. As she pours cat biscuits into his bowl, he pushes her hand aside and starts gobbling them up.

'You'll be sorry when you can't even jump high enough to get on my lap,' she says. She leaves the apartment before he can come back with a snappy reply.

She runs down the stairs two at a time.

At the bottom she only has a moment to register the two shadowed figures rushing at her, before she is pushed to the floor.

# 8

Katrina feels herself being rolled over, and then hands are tugging at her backpack, at the straps.

'Get off!' she screams and lashes out with a foot, kicking one of her assailants in the shin.

He leaps back, grabbing his leg, shouting, '*Filho da puta!*'

The other one laughs as he drags Katrina's rucksack off her back. She struggles to hold onto it, but then he has torn it from her grip. The other one joins him. Two young skinheads. Tattoos crawl down their arms and up their necks from underneath their white T-shirts. The one she kicked in the shin grins at her, exposing crooked brown teeth. He returns the favour, booting her in the side.

She yells in pain and curls up, thinking. *Just go, take my rucksack and leave me alone.*

Katrina hears the front door opening, and then an American man shouting, 'Hey! What's going on?'

She looks up to see a man running across the lobby. The two skinheads try to run past him, but he grabs one of them and swings him around, slamming him against the wall. The other one stops and grabs the American, who swings around and punches him in the stomach. As he crumples to the floor the first one aims a punch at his face. Katrina's rescuer easily deflects it and elbows him in the nose.

The skinhead staggers back, howling, his hand to his face. Blood drips from his nose and down his shirt. Katrina thinks, *He's got them now. They won't get away with my rucksack*.

But then the young man lying on the floor kicks his feet out in a scissor action around the American's ankles, and trips him up. He drops to the floor, hands out to break his fall, and the two skinheads dash out of the door, with Katrina's rucksack.

'Wait there!' the man shouts, scrambling to his feet. A moment later and he is gone too.

Katrina struggles to her knees, clutching her side. The pain is not too bad. The skinhead mistimed his kick; it could have been a lot worse. Pausing a moment before she attempts to stand up, she wonders if she will see her rucksack again.

Feeling faint, she decides against standing up for the moment, and shuffles over to the stairs and sits on the bottom step. She takes a deep breath to calm herself.

There was something odd about that man who rescued her, she realises, as she ponders over what has just happened. It takes her a moment, until she pins that thought down to his clothes. Wearing a light beige jacket, over a T-shirt and white slacks, he looked like he had stepped out of an episode of Miami Vice.

'Great,' Katrina says, her voice shockingly loud in the silence of the lobby. 'You've just been rescued by a fashion throwback to the eighties.'

* * *

Stahl chases the thugs down the street and around the corner into a cobbled, narrow side alley. The two men stop and turn around to face Stahl. The one with blood down his face and shirt starts swearing in Portuguese.

The American holds his hands up in a placatory gesture. 'Hey, I'm sorry. I got carried away, okay?'

The other skinhead, carrying the rucksack by its straps one-handed, walks up to Stahl and prods him in the chest with his index finger. 'You said a few bruises maybe, but look at him. You broke his nose, man!'

'Yeah, yeah, don't worry about it. He should be thanking me. A broken nose'll give him some serious street cred.'

The one with the broken nose struts up to Stahl, his face a mask of fury. 'I'll give you some street cred, man. I'll give you some street cred you'll never forget.'

'Yeah?' Stahl's voice drops an octave. 'You wanna dance with me? Let's do it, let's do it right here and now. We'll see who's got street cred then.'

Something in his eyes, in the tone of his voice, makes the two thugs step back. The one holding the rucksack throws it at Stahl, who catches it easily.

'Where's the rest of our money, man?'

Stahl opens up his wallet and pulls out a wad of bills. He throws the money at the skinheads, and the breeze catches the notes and sends them drifting down the alley.

'Don't spend it all at once,' he says.

Whilst the two thugs are chasing around, scrambling to pick up their money, Stahl quickly checks through the rucksack. He finds the handbag and opens it out, tipping the contents onto the stone cobbles.

'Damn it!' he hisses, not finding what he wants.

He quickly scoops everything back into the handbag and the rucksack, fastens it back up, and then leaves the skinheads still gathering their pay for the morning's work.

He turns the corner and begins walking back to the young woman's apartment block. Her knight in shining armour, rescuing her belongings at great personal risk. The morning might not be a complete loss, then. *After all*, he thinks, *she's an attractive young woman, and who knows how grateful she might be?*

Besides which, he also took the key to her apartment from her handbag. That USB stick has to be somewhere, and he will find it.

# 9

Katrina is sitting at the bottom of the stairs in her apartment building's lobby when her rescuer returns with her rucksack. He sees her, holds her rucksack up and grins. 'Looks like it's your lucky day.'

'Oh my gosh, thank you so much.' Katrina gets to her feet and takes the rucksack from him. 'I don't know how I can ever repay you.'

The American grins, and immediately Katrina is struck by his Hollywood handsomeness and his big, cheesy movie-star smile. And his outdated fashion sense. It's almost as though he is not real, as though he is a caricature. He reminds her of Don Johnson in *Miami Vice*.

'Don't worry about it. It makes my day to be able to rescue a beautiful damsel in distress.'

*Corny dialogue, too*, Katrina thinks.

'Well, I don't know about the beautiful, but I was certainly in distress.' Katrina unclips her rucksack and opens it up.

'I wouldn't worry about checking your things, they never got a chance to open it,' the American says. 'I should know. I was right behind them all the way.'

'Well, you can never be too sure.' Katrina pulls out her handbag and looks inside. 'Looks like everything's there, thank goodness.'

'I told you.'

Katrina returns the handbag to the rucksack, closes it and slings it over her shoulder. She puts out her hand to shake. 'Thank you ever so much. And I don't even know your name. Mine's Katrina.'

'Nice to meet you, Katrina. I'm Ben Stahl.' He takes her hand and gives it a single, powerful shake. Katrina can't help but think, *That is not the handshake of a person who is making friends. It's more of a power play, a signal that says, 'I'm the guy on top here, and don't you forget it.*'

'Well, thank you again. You were very brave to chase those two thugs outside like that. They didn't hurt you, did they?'

Stahl grins his big Hollywood smile, as though the very thought is ridiculous. 'Two young punks like that? No way. Once they saw me chasing them, they just dropped your rucksack and harum-scarumed outta here. I've never seen two kids run so fast.'

Katrina smiles. 'Good. I would have hated that you got into a fight with them again over my possessions. So, once again, thank you. You saved me a lot of hassle today. I don't know what I would have done if they had got away with my bag. But anyway, I really must be going, or else I'm going to be late for work.'

Stahl, still grinning, says nothing. He is blocking her exit, and Katrina is beginning to wonder if he will ever move, if maybe she will have to push her way past him, when he finally speaks.

'You know what? My car's just outside. I could give you a lift to work.'

'Oh no, thank you. You've done more than enough for me this morning. I don't want to take up any more of your time.'

'Hey, don't talk like that. I've got all the time in the world. And a pretty girl like you in my car, I'll feel like a million bucks. You'll be doing me the favour.'

Katrina glances at her watch. She is running late and, despite what Quinn might say, she's not sure how well Jay would look upon her being late two days in a row.

'Okay,' she says, finally. 'But no more favours after this, all right? Otherwise I'm going to be in your debt for the rest of my life.'

They step outside into the bright sunlight. For a moment Katrina hangs back, sure that the two thugs are waiting for them, ready to pounce. After the shock of Oliver Lowenstein collapsing in her arms last night, the news about the possibility that an Iranian hitman is stalking her, and now the attempted mugging this morning, Katrina's nerves are on a knife edge.

Stahl seems to sense her discomfort. 'Don't worry, those two punks aren't coming back. If they do, I'll see them off.'

Katrina smiles, to show him she is all right, and they walk down the street. She is relieved to see that traffic looks fairly light this morning, and is wondering if she should maybe go on the bus after all, when Stahl stops. The red sports car parked beside them blips, the headlights flashing, and Stahl bends down and opens the passenger door.

'Wow,' Katrina says. 'What a car.'

'A Chevrolet Corvette, the C6 model.' The American grins again, like a kid in a candy store. 'She's got 500 horsepower under her hood and goes like a hellcat.'

Inwardly, Katrina winces. She's still half-tempted to refuse the lift and catch the bus. But Stahl is standing in front of her, grinning that grin, and holding the door open for her. She can think of no way to refuse without causing offence.

She climbs into the car, placing her rucksack on her lap. Stahl climbs in, switches on the engine, and flips a switch. The roof lifts back smoothly, folding up into the boot. With the briefest of glances behind, to check for other cars, Stahl accelerates the car out of its parking space, and slots into a space in the fast-moving traffic.

Stahl drives aggressively. Katrina clutches her rucksack as he overtakes other vehicles, and swerves into gaps in between cars that she wouldn't think possible.

'Where do you want dropping off?' Stahl shouts over the roar of the city traffic.

'Guanabara Bay, please.'

Soon they are on a freeway, and Katrina begins to relax a little. The wind is blowing through her hair, and the delights of being in an open-top sports car, beneath the glorious blue sky and the warm morning sun, beats the pants off travelling to work on one of Rio's buses. Even an air conditioned one.

Katrina sits back and decides to enjoy the ride.

* * *

Stahl hadn't been kidding; he really does feel like a million bucks. Like all his lottery numbers have come up at once. Driving through sunny Rio in a Corvette C6, the roof down, a beautiful girl in the passenger seat, what red-blooded man wouldn't feel good about himself? He glances down at her exposed thigh, and likes what he sees. He just wishes she wasn't clutching that damned rucksack to herself. He could've seen more of her curves.

*Got to keep your mind on the job, though*, he thinks. *Maybe later, when I've sorted this mess out, then we can get down to some rest and relaxation. With a little bit of persuasion, she looks like she might be up for anything.*

His plan is to drop her off at work and then head straight back to her apartment. Giving her a lift was a masterstroke, he has to admit to himself. This way he knows exactly where she is, and he can take his time searching the apartment.

And once he's found what he wants, then he can take a little time out to explore those curves he's currently thinking about, that are hidden behind her rucksack.

That will be a nice little diversion, a very nice little diversion indeed.

# 10

Jay looks up from his computer as he hears the car screeching to a halt outside. He walks over to his office door and looks in the waiting room, something he has been avoiding doing for the last ten minutes. The nine Chilean rugby players have also turned towards the noise, interrupting their impromptu training session. Quinn is standing posed like a statue in the middle of the room, surrounded by the Chileans. Her feet are planted wide apart on the carpet, and she is holding the rugby ball over her head.

Jay would like to whistle his admiration at the beautiful, striking sight she presents. But if he does, he is sure he will have to dodge a rugby-ball-shaped missile aimed right at his head.

Jay has almost asked the rugby players to stop their 'training session' on two occasions, especially when they came perilously close to knocking over his glass shelves of awards. Some of the awards are many years old, stretching back to his early teens, when his life consisted of little more than surfing. Most summer weekends back then had been taken up with entering surfing competitions, and he collected quite a gallery of medals and winners' cups.

On that shelf are other prizes for triathlons, marathon runs, and climbing. There are also certificates of competency regarding his licences to take people diving, surfing, caving, rock climbing and skydiving. Jay feels very attached to the contents of those shelves.

But the rugby players are unstoppable. Each and every one takes up the space of a small mountain. It hasn't helped that they are completely besotted with Quinn, who has enthusiastically joined in with their game. When she first greeted them as they arrived, barefoot in a pair of cut-off jeans riding so high on her thighs her buttocks are peeking out from under them, and in a cropped, skin-tight T-shirt, the Chileans' jaws collectively dropped to the floor.

It didn't take long for the fun to start. They have been passing a rugby ball to each other, shouting commands in Chilean, and sometimes leaping over furniture or diving to the floor and rolling over. Every time they do this, the shelves rattle, and Jay closes his eyes, waiting for the inevitable crash of glass and metal. So, when Jay hears the car skidding to an abrupt halt outside, it's the perfect excuse for him to go out and investigate.

The Australian wonders if lack of sleep is befuddling his brain as he sees Katrina climbing out of the passenger side of a red sports car, driven, it seems, by Don Johnson. The *Miami Vice* guy flashes his perfectly straight white teeth at Katrina in a big grin and raises a hand in farewell. 'It's been real, Katrina. Have a great day, now.' He spins the Corvette round in a tight circle, narrowly missing Jay's beat-up truck, and speeds out of the car park.

'Who's that?' Jay says.

Katrina, eyes hidden by her sunglasses, rucksack slung over her shoulder, saunters past him, without giving him a glance. 'Oh, no one. Just someone who offered me a lift into work this morning, that's all.'

*What's going on?* Jay thinks as he watches her walking towards the office. *I only left her just over two hours ago. When did she pick this guy up?* Jay glances back at the car, just in time to see it disappear round a bend. Thinking about it now, Jay is fairly sure he has seen the American before. But just where and when eludes him.

Right now, though, he doesn't pursue that line of thinking, as he is suddenly consumed with jealousy. The thought of Katrina being given a lift into work by a flashy guy like that, and the look on her face as she sauntered past him, makes Jay wonder if he was too hard on her yesterday. He had been angry with her for turning up late, but had it really been fair to set her to looking at the office accounts? Jay wonders now if part of his displeasure had been at the fact that she never seems interested in him. Can't she see how he feels about her? Especially after last night, walking the streets of Rio, talking until the dawn. Most girls would have been putty in his hands by then, but not her. Every time he draws close, she backs off. Not only that, but the shutters come crashing down, and Jay feels as though he has been slapped in the face. Which was exactly what happened last night. And then, this morning she comes to work with *that* guy!

Jay thoughts are interrupted as he hears a roar of approval from his office, and then Katrina's small scream of surprise. She appears in the doorway, whipping off her sunglasses. 'I'm guessing those are the nine Chilean rugby players you mentioned?'

Jay nods. 'This is going to be an interesting morning.'

* * *

Stahl stands outside Katrina's apartment, his face only inches from the door. He is a professional, and knows that he needs to be single-minded in everything he does. This is how he has reached so far in his career, by being completely focused on his work. He lets nothing distract him from the job at hand.

Nothing.

This is the reason his is standing in front of the door, his face almost up against the wooden panels, taking slow, deep breaths, and trying to clear his mind. Especially of the blond surfer dude. Stahl finds it hard to believe that Katrina would work for such an empty-headed beach bum. The thought that it might be worse than that, that they might actually be sleeping together, is beyond his capabilities to dwell on too much. If he does, he might just turn around, get back in the car, and drive back to Guanabaro Bay, where he can deliver a swift bullet straight to surfer dude's head.

Right between the eyes. Yeah, that would teach him.

Stahl closes his eyes, takes a deep breath, holds it, and then exhales slowly. With that breath go all thoughts about surfer dude. He can take care of him later. Now he is focused on the job once more, Stahl slips the key into the lock and opens the door.

*This is going to be sweet*, he thinks, as he closes the door behind him. He places his briefcase on the floor and snaps open the locks. Inside the case is a pack of rubber gloves and a laptop. Strapped inside the lid is a handgun, a SIG Sauer P220 fitted with a silencer. Slipping off his jacket and placing it over a chair, Stahl then takes out a pair of the gloves and pulls them on. He wipes the apartment key and door handle, removing his fingerprints.

Before he does anything else he takes a good look at his surroundings. The apartment is tiny. He is standing in the main room, a combination living room, dining area and kitchen. The kitchen is small, the counter cluttered with a kettle, a microwave, a toaster and a sink. An oven and a fridge fill up the rest of the kitchen. There is a table, with just enough room to seat four people around it, and a small, two-seater settee. In a corner on a table there is a tiny, battered portable television. Stahl hasn't seen one of those in years. A wooden set of shelves stands against the remaining wall.

Stahl picks up the photograph he spies there of Katrina and a young man, arms wrapped around each other, on a beach. They are both smiling happily. Stahl briefly wonders where the man is now, before putting the photograph back in its place. He decides to investigate Katrina, to find out a little more about her.

Returning to his briefcase, he pulls out the laptop and boots it up. He opens up a web browser and types Katrina's name into a news search engine. Five minutes later of trawling through news stories he has found what he wants. It seems Katrina has been running from her past, from the tragic loss of her boyfriend in a terrible skydiving accident. The American smiles. Maybe he can use that information to his advantage at some point. The emotionally damaged women are always the most easily manipulated, he finds. He closes the laptop and slips it back into his briefcase.

He is returning to continue searching the room when he hears a sound behind him, and spins around, hands up ready to fight. He is cursing his stupidity at leaving his gun in the open case, in plain view. But the gun is still there, in its case, and he can see nobody else in the room. Just as his body is slowly beginning to relax, he hears the noise again. This time he sees the cat as it runs from behind the settee, leaps up onto a windowsill and scrambles out through a window, locked open just wide enough for the cat to fit through.

Stahl waits for his pulse to slow down, and then walks over to the window and shuts it. He hates cats, and hopes this one gets run over before it decides to return. After allowing his pulse rate to return to normal, he begins methodically working his way through the room, looking in the cupboards, under furniture, beneath the settee's cushions, everywhere he can think of that Katrina might have hidden the USB stick. Once he has exhausted all possible hiding places in the main living area, he moves into the bedroom.

He is surprised to see a double bed in here, along with a chest of drawers and a tiny wardrobe. There is hardly any floor space left, the room is so full with just these three items of furniture. He takes the drawers first, opening them one by one and carefully sifting through the contents. He searches the wardrobe, under the bed and the mattress, all the while growing more impatient and frustrated. A thought is growing in his mind — a horrible suspicion that he is wrong, and that Katrina does not have the USB stick after all.

Stahl sits on the edge of the bed and checks his watch. He has plenty of time.

Now that the thought has surfaced in his mind, he needs to think about it for a while. He lies down on the bed, crossing his arms over his chest and closing his eyes.

Lowenstein had the USB stick before he entered the Baronetti, of this Stahl is utterly certain. But then he did not have it on him when he was laid out on the table having his heart attack. Where, then, could it be? At what point could he have removed it from his person, and where could he have put it? The American is reasonably sure he did not drop it in the club. He can't be a hundred percent, but if so, he is certain it would have been found by now, and the game would be over.

No, Lowenstein collapsed against Katrina, and he had the USB stick in his hand. He had to have passed it to her; it can't have gone anywhere else. Has she already given it to the police? Is that why Benzali was here this morning? Did she find the USB stick in her bag and call him?

Stahl's hands curl into fists as he recalls watching the detective leave the building, all the time having what he, Stahl, has come all this way to retrieve. Is it that simple? Has he been chasing a dead end? Perhaps he should go and visit the detective soon. He just has time for a conversation with Benzali before he heads back to Guanabara Bay and offers Katrina a lift home. That way he can slip her key back into her bag before she notices it is missing.

And maybe he can get a proper thank you from her, for fighting off those two thugs. Maybe she could thank him right here in this bed.

* * *

Katrina never tires of the experience of slipping underwater. After rolling backwards off the boat and under the surface of the South Atlantic, she rights herself and begins sweeping her fins in an up-and-down stroke to propel herself deeper. Jay disappeared beneath the waves first, followed by the rugby players, and she is at the rear.

She pulls herself along the line they have attached to the wreck of the *Cavo Artemidi*, with a buoy as a marker on the surface. Deeper and deeper she dives, following the last of the rugby players only a few feet below her. Jay is worried about this dive, she can tell. He has to be one of the most laid-back men she has ever met, but this morning he is tense. Part of it, she is sure, is down to their lack of sleep. But the other part is the attitude of the rugby players. They are loud and wild and virtually uncontrollable. Jay has had to repeat instructions several times, and stress the importance of following his lead down below. The Chileans have all been diving before, and that is simultaneously a good and bad thing. Good, because he doesn't have to teach them any new skills, or hold their hands underwater. Bad, because they presume they know enough not to have to listen to him.

Out on the boat, the buoy bobbing

up and down beside them on the waves, he debated with Katrina about cancelling the whole dive, and refunding them their money.

'I'm not sure that's a good idea,' Katrina whispered, as the Chileans began chanting yet another rugby song. 'Not only is that a lot of money to refund, but you'll put their backs up big-time.'

They both looked over at Osvaldo, sitting at the wheel, a cigarette dangling from his mouth. No one knows Osvaldo's age, but Katrina reckons he has to be at least ninety. The old man is sprightly, for sure. He can handle a boat in all kinds of weather, and Katrina once watched in amazement as he performed twenty-one armed press-ups on each arm for the amusement of the local kids. But he is small and scrawny, and no use in a fight if the rugby players decided to cut up rough.

'Katrina, if we have an incident down there — and God forbid one of these drongos gets himself in a tight spot — we could be in a lot of trouble.'

‘Maybe you could try laying down the law, threatening to call it all off, and just see how they react.’

That’s what Jay did. He stomped up and down the boat, threatening to take them back, shouting, pointing, swearing, waving his arms so wildly that Katrina thought he might fall overboard. And it worked. The rugby players calmed down enough to listen to one last set of instructions, and get themselves in the water without a hitch.

Katrina can see them gathering by the wreck now, waiting until they are all grouped together again. Jay gives her the OK sign, index finger and thumb touching to form a circle, with the other fingers extended. Katrina relaxes a little, knowing that Jay is happier now.

On a signal from Jay they swim alongside the wreck’s barnacle-encrusted hull, over kelp forests and the rocky protrusions of the seabed. A school of black durgon and triggerfish glide towards them, apparently curious to see what is going on.

Katrina pauses to have a good look around. Marine life of all shapes and sizes darts to and fro. She sees a blackbar soldierfish, its mouth turned down in its characteristic grumpy expression. Another school of fish approaches, this time butterflyfish. Queen angelfish flit up close to her and then away.

Katrina looks down as she glides through the warm water, and spies a red rock crab clinging, almost invisible, to a kelp-covered rock. Beside him, emerging from their hiding places, she sees two brown spiny lobsters. Katrina feels almost giddy at the sight of all this ocean life; and when she looks up again, what she sees takes her breath away.

A mobula ray glides over them, highlighted by rays of sunshine refracted through the water. Katrina feels she has never been happier and more fulfilled than at this moment. She glances over at Jay, who has also seen the ray and is pointing it out to the Chileans. Some of them have underwater cameras, and start snapping off shots.

Jay looks at Katrina and gives her the OK signal again. Katrina returns the signal, and experiences a sudden rush of . . . what? Love? Affection? Is she falling in love with Jay? Can that be even possible, after everything she has been through?

No, *I'm not falling in love with this man. I can't. The only reason I am having these feelings is because of the time we spent together last night, talking. Because I am tired and emotional, after seeing Oliver Lowenstein die in my arms. I'm just being a silly little girl, acting like an infatuated teenager. It's nothing more than that.*

But is that all there is to it? When she thinks about it, there have been plenty of moments over the last few months when she has caught Jay looking at her in a certain way. She has always just shrugged it off, never taking it seriously. What would a handsome, laid-back guy like him see in her? Jay can have his pick of any girl he wants, she has always believed, and last night's conversation went some way to confirming that thought.

But today, again, after spending last night talking with Jay, Katrina is beginning to wonder if perhaps she has been too wrapped up in her memories of Pete. She lives so much in the past, mourning her lost love, that maybe she is failing to see what is right in front of her eyes. Could it be that Quinn is right, after all? She might not be the hottest girl in town, but Jay might think more of her than she has realised so far.

Her thoughts are broken when she realises the teeming ocean life is rapidly disappearing. The ray has gone, and the school of durgon and triggerfish is swimming away. Katrina looks at Jay, who suddenly seems tense and unhappy again. He slowly raises a hand and points behind her.

She turns and looks up, and behind. A cold fist grabs her insides and twists.

A mako shark is swimming towards them, tiny flicks of its tail propelling it through the water, its mouth open, revealing its jagged lines of teeth.

# 11

Benzali replaces the telephone in its cradle and sits back, mulling over the conversation he has just had. It is never pleasant breaking the bad news of a person's death to a friend or family member, especially over the telephone. But Benzali had to let the US politician, McCluskey, know of Lowenstein's fatal heart attack as soon as possible, so that he could arrange to meet him. The politician had taken the news badly, but had promised to meet the detective later that afternoon.

Benzali is not a man who appreciates a good mystery, unlike the fictional detectives in the books that his wife devours. Sherlock Holmes would have solved the case by now, but Benzali is not possessed of that famous detective's legendary, if fictional, intuition.

No, for Benzali, this case will be

solved through dogged police work: chasing up leads, questioning everyone involved, and writing up his reports, carefully and methodically. The solution to the mystery might be ordinary and dull, with no sinister overtones at all.

But Benzali suspects otherwise.

The telephone rings and the detective picks up the receiver. 'Hello, Detective Benzali speaking.'

'Detective Benzali, I am so pleased I caught you. I'm sure you are a busy man, but I feel it might be in both of our interests to meet up.'

'Who am I speaking to?'

'Ben Stahl. I'm with the CIA, and I am investigating the murder of Oliver Lowenstein.'

'Murder?'

'Yes, I'm afraid so, Detective. We firmly believe that the professor may have been murdered for the information he was carrying. I really don't want to have to go through this on the telephone; it would be much better if we could meet up. Perhaps we could meet at Katrina Maslow's apartment in, say, half an hour? I have discovered something which will be of great interest to you, and I believe you have some information we will find invaluable in our investigation.'

Benzali is intrigued, although not entirely convinced by the American's manner. Nevertheless, he agrees to meet, and replaces the telephone on his desk.

How strange that the CIA has become involved in the riddle of Lowenstein's fatal visit to the Baronetti. Benzali is looking forward to going home tonight and relating the day's proceedings to his wife. This will take her nose out of her books for once. A real life mystery, worthy perhaps of Sherlock Holmes.

Benzali wonders what fresh light the CIA operative, Stahl, can throw on this puzzle. After all, nothing about this case makes any immediate sense to the detective. An old man, a scientist, who should have been at home, stumbles into a night club and dies of a heart attack. But not before mentioning two names: one of them a young woman, who has no apparent connection to him, and the other a notorious Iranian hitman, who is dead.

The scientist was on the run with important information, and Benzali is convinced that Lowenstein has to have given something to Katrina in that moment when he collapsed in her arms at the Baronetti, or earlier in the day when they met on the bus. This is the only reason Benzali can think of that he would mention the young woman's name.

Or perhaps the answer is less complicated. Perhaps he was simply an infatuated old man, and the pursuit of that infatuation led to his heart attack.

But then why the mention of Kubaschi? Has the hitman crawled from the grave, returning from the dead like some zombie from a horror film, to hunt down the English professor?

No, not possible. Benzali is a

practical man, dismissing ghost stories and superstitions as blatant nonsense. The answer, he feels, lies in the information the old man stole from Coeus Petroleum. He has to have given it to Katrina, Benzali is convinced of this. But if so, the young woman obviously has no idea where it might be, or what it is.

And now this telephone call from Stahl, who seems to think he and Benzali might be in a position to share information. *If this is true, and we pool our resources*, the detective thinks, *we might get to the bottom of the mystery much quicker*. Stahl was eager to meet up at Katrina Maslow's apartment. The detective hopes that the young woman is not in trouble with the American forces of law. He took quite a shine to her this morning, and feels a fatherly protection towards her.

Deciding it is best not to keep the American waiting, Benzali switches on his answer machine and leaves the office.

* * *

Katrina is frozen solid with fear as she watches the shark swim in slow, lazy circles in front of them. It is almost as though the mako is putting on a show, delaying the moment at which it will attack, like a cat playing with a mouse. She wonders if sharks have a way of communicating with other sharks; if right now this one is sending signals to its mates, and soon they will be surrounded by hundreds of hungry predators ready to rip them apart in an orgy of teeth and flesh.

*Concentrate*, Katrina thinks. *Concentrate on what you are doing*.

Aware that she is breathing too fast — that not only is she in danger of hyperventilating and suffering a dizzy spell, but that she will also quickly run out of air at this rate — Katrina begins to slow her breathing. The adrenalin rush of seeing the shark and the primal instinct to flee flooding her body need to be controlled. The young woman knows enough to realise that if she turns her back on the predator and attempts to swim away, she will be eaten. This is the shark's natural domain: he is king of his element, the ocean, and Katrina knows she is the intruder. They have to think cleverly if they are to stay alive.

The first rule of survival when confronted with a shark, Katrina knows, is never take your eyes off it. She needs to keep it in her field of vision all the time and prevent it from swimming around her, and sneaking an attack upon her.

Katrina begins the difficult task of finning slowly backwards. She knows she is not far from the rest of the group, and that they will have more safety in numbers as long as they all work together.

The shark continues swimming in its tight circles, still not seeming ready to attack. Katrina feels hands pulling at her legs, drawing her in close to the group. Jay has organised the Chileans, their backs up against the rusted hull of the *Cavo Artemidi*. This way the shark can only attack them from one direction, and they can keep it in view at all times.

Jay looks up and down the line of rugby players, who are all staring intently at the mako. He makes fists with both hands out in front of him, extends his index fingers, and then brings them together side-by-side.

*Stay together*.

The mako swims closer, obviously intrigued by the collection of divers. Although rigid with fear, Katrina still cannot help but marvel at the fish's beauty. She estimates that this one is about ten feet long. It is coloured a brilliant metallic blue along its top length, and white underneath. Its eyes are black, like a doll's eyes, and it has a long snout above those jagged lines of teeth.

The shark swims towards one of the rugby players at the end of the group. Katrina can see he is breathing rapidly, far too fast, as he clings to the barnacles on the hull of the wreck. The mako nudges him with its snout, and then swims away. The rugby player looks as though he is trembling, and Katrina is worried that he will suddenly make a break for it, and try and swim back to the boat.

If he does that, he is dead. No one can out-swim a shark, and the mako will be attracted by his swimming motion. The shark will catch up with him in seconds, and its teeth will tear his diving suit into shreds, along with the Chilean. Then the water will fill with blood, and the shark will go into a feeding frenzy, and none of them will have a chance of surviving.

The mako is returning, heading straight back for the rugby player, almost as though it can sense he is the weakest of the pack. It butts its snout against his chest a couple of times, seemingly sizing him up as a potential meal. The shark turns and swims away again, but they all know it will be back.

Katrina looks at Jay. He points at her and holds out his hand, palm facing down, and raises and lowers it twice.

*Stay here*.

Jay begins swimming towards the distressed rugby player. Katrina and all the Chileans watch him as he glides to the end of the line.

The shark is returning.

Jay crouches by the Chilean. He is shaking his head and looking ready to flee as the shark swims closer. Katrina, close to panicking, tries to remember the rules for surviving a shark encounter. There aren't many.

Keep the shark in view at all times.

Place your back against an object so that you can only be attacked from the front.

If the shark attacks, hit it on the snout or poke it in the eyes.

Last, and most obvious of all: get out of the water as soon as possible.

The mako approaches silently, and butts its snout up against the rugby player's chest. Jay pulls his respirator out of his mouth and holds it up in front of the shark, sending a burst of bubbles over its eyes, mouth and gills. The shark immediately turns in a jerky, spasmodic motion, and swims away with deep, powerful thrusts of its tail.

Jay sticks his thumb up.

*Go up.*

No one needs telling twice. They are diving in relatively shallow water and have not been down long, so they have no need to worry about suffering from the bends. As Katrina swims up, she keeps a constant lookout for the return of the shark. Now is the most dangerous time. They are all unprepared for an attack, and it could come at any moment, from any direction.

When she breaks the surface of the sea, Osvaldo is already helping pull the rugby players from the water. Jay, she notes, is still in the ocean, helping the Chileans get handholds on the ladder attached to the side of the boat, helping them up. Katrina is suddenly so very proud of him for making sure everyone else is safe before he leaves the water. He beckons her over as the last one clambers up the ladder.

'Quick! Come on, get on the boat!'

As she reaches him he grabs her arm and hauls her over to the ladder. She grabs hold of the first rung, just as a cry of alarm is raised from the deck above them.

*'Tubaryo! Tubaryo!'*

Katrina twists her head and sees a shark fin slicing through the waves towards them. All of her strength seems to drain from her body, but she reaches up and pulls herself up the ladder. As she leaves the water, the scuba tank on her back becomes a lead weight, dragging her down. Jay is right behind her, pushing her, shoving her up.

Hands reach out and drag Katrina on board, and she tumbles down on the deck. As she turns to see if Jay is on the boat yet, he scrambles over the side, surrounded by the Chileans, who are helping to haul him on board.

Jay pulls off his mask and helps

Katrina off with hers. For a few moments they look into each other's eyes, and then he starts laughing. Before she knows it she has started giggling too, as relief that their ordeal is now finished overwhelms her.

The Chileans start laughing too, and then they start clapping their hands and singing a song. Osvaldo guns the boat's engine into life and heads back for shore. Katrina remains sitting on the deck, gazing up at the blue sky, feeling the swell of the ocean beneath her, and is glad to be alive.

# 12

As Detective Benzali stands on the pavement outside Katrina's apartment block, waiting for Stahl, he starts to wonder what the CIA's involvement in this affair could be. Benzali's gut is telling him that something is wrong, and he is a man who believes in intuition.

The information he has received about Oliver Lowenstein and his project from Coeus Petroleum has been vague. Despite being put through to several different departments, no one could actually tell Benzali what it was that Lowenstein had been working on. For some it just seemed they were not high enough up the ladder to be told this information, whilst others had muttered about 'a top-secret project' and a 'need-to-know basis'. Nothing that Benzali said could convince them he needed to know, despite the fact that it surely had to have a bearing on the case.

But, Benzali knows, it doesn't take a genius to link Lowenstein's visit with the upcoming climate conference. His chat with Katrina confirmed that suspicion, and now Benzali is keen to know what information Lowenstein had in his possession, and where it might be. They have already searched his hotel room and his luggage. The man had been travelling light, and Benzali has a feeling that he had not expected to be returning home.

'Detective Benzali! What a pleasure to meet you!'

The policeman turns, startled at the sound of the American's voice. He had obviously been deep in thought to allow himself to be sneaked up on like that. The American is holding out his hand, ready to shake. Benzali is surprised at his choice of clothing, which seems garish and outdated. But, other than that, he is good-looking in a film-star kind of way, and he is smiling confidently, showing off his perfectly white, perfectly regular teeth.

Benzali notices that the smile does not extend to his eyes.

The two men shake hands.

'Stahl, Ben Stahl. Pleased you could take time out of your busy schedule to meet me.'

'Always a pleasure to help our cousins in the north,' Benzali says.

Stahl laughs, but again Benzali detects no warmth or humour in that laugh.

'Let's go inside, shall we? I have something to show you.' Stahl holds out his arm, indicating that the detective should go before him.

They enter the cool lobby and head for the stairs, taking them two at a time. They stop outside Katrina's door.

'Don't we need to inform the building supervisor, or do you have a key?' the detective says.

Stahl grins. 'I'm with the CIA, Detective. Of course I have a key.' With a showman's flourish he produces a key from his pocket and throws it up in the air. Benzali watches it spin for a moment before the American snatches it in mid-flight. 'Detective, I have a few questions for you before we go inside.'

Benzali nods. 'Yes?'

'When you visited Katrina Maslow this morning, I am assuming it had to do with the Oliver Lowenstein affair?'

Benzali is tempted to smile at this turn of phrase, but he has the feeling that the CIA operative would not take it well. Stahl, it seems to the detective, has an inflated sense of his own importance.

'Mr Stahl, I will happily share such knowledge as I have, once I see your CIA credentials.' Benzali shrugs and smiles. 'I am sorry to trouble you, but I am sure you understand.'

'Of course.' Stahl grins and pulls a battered leather wallet from his back pocket, flips it open and holds it up for Benzali to inspect.

There seems to be nothing wrong with the ID, but Benzali's sense of unease is growing. His intuition is telling him that something is wrong with the American, and that he is not all he says he is.

'Thank you,' Benzali says.

'Detective.' Stahl lowers his voice and steps closer, as though he is speaking in confidence. 'I know nothing of your past dealings with the CIA, or if you have a grudge against the organisation, but you seem rather reticent to deal with me. However, I am asking you now, as one peace officer to another, to put aside any past grudges you may hold. This situation is far too important for us to be withholding information from each other. Do I make myself clear?'

'Of course.'

'Good, good.' Stahl smiles his humourless grin again. 'Now, your visit with Miss Maslow this morning. Can I ask its purpose?'

'It is obvious, really. There is no mystery. I am heading the investigation into Mr Lowenstein's death, and felt it appropriate to continue my questioning of Katrina, after the incident in the night club.'

'And did Miss Maslow offer you anything?'

Benzali smiles, unable to resist. 'Yes, she did. A cup of coffee, and it was very nice coffee, too.'

'That's very funny, Detective, but I think you understand what I am asking you.'

'Are you asking me, did the professor give her something in the bar, which she then gave to me?'

The American's eyes narrow as he regards Benzali. 'Yes, we know that Lowenstein was in possession of some very important information, and that he may have given it to Miss Maslow.'

Benzali spreads his hands out. 'The young woman I interviewed was upset by the old man's death, nothing more. She has no knowledge of anything the professor might have had on him, and he gave her nothing.'

'In which case, our business is almost done.' Stahl inserts the key into the door's lock. 'Just one last thing.' He opens the door and gestures for Benzali to proceed first.

The detective enters the apartment, stopping just over the threshold as he sees the heavy-duty tarpaulin covering the floor. He has a fraction of a moment in which he realises the trap he has fallen into, before Stahl plants a hand on his back and shoves him into middle of the room.

Benzali stumbles and turns. Stahl has shut the door and is aiming a gun at his chest.

'You'll never get away with this,' Benzali says.

'Oh, I think I will,' Stahl replies.

# 13

Katrina laughs as she watches Quinn being carried around on the rugby players' shoulders, the men singing a Chilean song of celebration. Although their dive was cut short, they seem to feel they have had full value for money by surviving a shark attack.

'I don't understand. I thought they would have wanted a refund. We were hardly down there any time at all,' Katrina says.

Jay stops hauling the scuba gear out of the pickup to watch the Chileans for a moment. 'Nah, they've had a great time. Imagine how often they can dine out on that story from now on, especially after the tale's been embellished in the telling a few times.'

'I guess you're right. Look at them go.'

The rugby players are now running

around the car park, holding a screaming, giggling Quinn high over their heads. As they continue to celebrate, Katrina helps Jay carry the scuba gear into the storage locker where they can clean it, perform some basic maintenance, and refill the tanks with air.

As they stack the tanks together, Katrina glances over at Jay, the muscles on his arms standing out as he carries another oxygen bottle inside. She thinks back to last night, and how Jay looked after her, refusing to let her go back to her apartment by herself after the shock she had in the Baronetti.

*He's good-looking, sensitive, strong and brave. What more could a girl ask for?* she thinks. *And, if I can believe what Quinn tells me, he likes me, too.*

'Hey,' she says. 'You were pretty damn fantastic down there, you know that?'

Jay smiles. 'Gotta look after the customers. If one gets eaten, word tends to get around. Bad for business, you know.'

'No, I'm serious. We all owe you our lives. Once he'd bitten one of us, that shark would've gone into a feeding frenzy. Who knows how many of us he would've chewed up before he got bored?'

'Yeah, well, you did all right yourself, you know that?' Jay puts the tank down and walks over to Katrina. 'You were exceptionally calm down there, which is no mean feat when coming face-to-face with a man-eater. And finning backwards — man, that was impressive. Where did you learn that particular skill?'

'Oh, my boyfriend taught me.'

'Yeah? He must be a pretty good diver. Not many divers can do that, propel yourself backwards through the water.' Jay looks at her, and Katrina feels as though she might wilt under his gaze. The unspoken question sits between them, *Are you and this guy still an item?*

Katrina thinks back to last night, when he had tried asking her if she was with anybody. She hadn't been able to answer him then, and again she finds herself unable to talk to him. Whenever the subject comes up, whenever she feels that attraction to Jay, and sees the possibility that he might be attracted to her, it's as though her emotions seize up. Katrina has to resist the urge to turn and flee, run out of the door and never come back.

Katrina feels she needs to tell Jay everything, to unburden herself of the grief and overwhelming sadness she still experiences every single day. But it is as though she is paralyzed by her memories of Pete, of the day he died. Katrina has travelled around the world, trying to escape, attempting to make a new life for herself. But no matter how far she travels, that awful day is always there with her. Katrina has visited some amazing places, seen beautiful vistas and met fascinating people in different cultures, but every day she still sees her fiancé plummeting to his death over the Kent countryside.

So far, Katrina has always accepted that she never had a choice, that she was simply destined to live her life mourning her boyfriend. But now, looking at Jay, she wonders if maybe she does have a choice, after all.

*Can't stay sad forever, babe*, she remembers Quinn telling her.

And maybe she's right.

Maybe she can start again.

All of these thoughts have flooded through Katrina's mind in an instant. She realises that Jay is waiting for her to say something, that at any moment he might turn away and start stacking the scuba gear again.

Katrina reaches out a trembling hand, suddenly needing to touch him — just to feel his hand in hers, his fingers entwined amongst her fingers. She wonders what it might feel like to embrace him, to hold him tight and kiss him.

'Jay, I . . . '

The Chileans barge between them, still carrying a screaming Quinn, and still singing their song of celebration. Katrina and Jay are pushed apart, and then a hand darts out and grabs Katrina and she is hauled away, pulled along by the rugby players as they head outside to start another circuit of the car park.

Katrina glances through the open door of the storage bay as she is dragged outside, and her heart aches as she sees Jay standing all alone inside, watching them head away.

'Help me!' Quinn shouts. 'Somebody rescue me from these crazy galoots!'

Even though Katrina is hurting inside, she still can't help laughing at Quinn.

*She doesn't much look like she needs rescuing*, thinks Katrina. *Not if that big, goofy grin on her face is anything to go by.*

* * *

Stahl wraps Benzali's body up in the heavy-duty tarpaulin. As he works he whistles a half-remembered tune from his childhood. His mother loved the old Rodgers and Hammerstein musicals. She had all the albums and would play them endlessly on her old record player, the music accompanied by an undertone of hissing and crackling because they had been played so often. The jaunty little tune he is whistling snatches of is probably one of theirs, but he can't put a name to it.

He has done his best to forget as much as he can about his family, his mother and father and two sisters, ever since the fire that took their lives. The neighbours all thought it was such a terrible tragedy and marvelled at the young boy's incredible luck, that he alone had been saved. But for Stahl, luck had never come into it. He had found his lifetime's passion that night: a predilection for murder. He had always hated his family. As far back as he could remember having conscious thoughts, he had despised them. And so once he had done away with them, he had set about trying to forget them.

But the tunes . . . He can never completely forget those, and somehow he has grown to love them. Whenever he does something of which he is particularly proud, he soon begins whistling.

And having the foresight to carpet Katrina's apartment with the tarpaulin before luring the detective in and murdering him . . . well, that was a stroke of genius. No mess to clean up, and all that blood would have taken hours of scrubbing. Now, being able to simply fold the tarpaulin over the policeman's body, it is all so simple.

Stahl uses thick electrician's tape to seal the tarpaulin up, and when he has finished he stands back and admires his work. Stahl can see the detective's face distorted through the clear plastic, and for a moment the American feels unsettled.

He walks around to the dead man's feet, grabs him by the ankles, and drags the body through to Katrina's bedroom. There, he shoves the dead detective under the bed and stands up. From this angle he can't see under the bed. The only way Benzali's corpse will be discovered is if Katrina kneels down and looks under the bed.

Stahl looks at his watch and decides to head on back to *J Stone Adventure Trips*, and see if Katrina wants a lift back home. He is growing impatient. If he can't find the USB stick by tomorrow he is going to call the whole thing off. But not before finding some compensation for his wasted trip.

Stahl looks at Katrina's double bed. He knows exactly what kind of compensation he wants.

# 14

Katrina breathes a deep sigh of relief once the Chilean rugby players have gone. They were fun, but they were exhausting, too. Quinn has staggered inside and fallen into her chair.

'Woohoo!' she yells, gazing up at Katrina and grinning. Her hair is in a tangle, and her short T-shirt has ridden up her torso, exposing her brown stomach.

'You'd better sort yourself out before Enrique sees you, or he might get jealous.'

'Why? You think he'd have liked being carried round the car park by a team of rugby players? I don't know if you've noticed, hun, but Enrique ain't that kind of guy.'

Katrina laughs. 'Don't be an idiot.' She hauls Quinn to her feet and pulls her T-shirt straight, then pushes her back into the chair. She grabs a brush and goes to work on her hair.

Quinn tries to push Katrina's hand away, but she is still weak with the excitement. 'Thanks, babe, but I can sort myself out.'

'No you can't, not right now. You look as though you tangled with that shark we met. When's Enrique coming to pick you up?'

'He ain't, tonight. He's meeting with his new best friends while they plan their next protest.'

'Okay, great. You can come back with me on the bus. Maybe we can have another girls' night out.' Katrina glances over at Jay, out in the car park, hosing down the wetsuits. What she really wants to do is find out what plans he has for tonight, and suggest that maybe they could go out for a drink.

But, ever since they were interrupted by the Chileans earlier, Katrina seems to have lost her nerve and her certainty of how she feels. It is as though she has been torn in two and become a split personality. One half is telling her to go for it — that Pete would want her to move on and forget that terrible day — whilst the other half feels that becoming romantically involved with another man would be a betrayal of Pete and everything they had together.

Jay also seems to have lost his nerve. He has spent the rest of the afternoon cleaning down the scuba gear with an intensity the job does not really need. Perhaps Quinn is mistaken, and Jay has no feelings for her in any romantic way. Maybe he realised Katrina's intentions in that moment before they were torn apart, and is now keeping out of her way, embarrassed at the thought of her declaring her feelings for him.

'Ouch!' Quinn grabs the hair brush off Katrina. 'What you doing, girl? You trying to scalp me or something?'

'Sorry. I was a million miles away.'

Quinn glances over at Jay. 'Yeah, I know exactly where you was, girl.'

Before Katrina can say anything else, they are interrupted as a man and a woman enter the office. They both look like holiday-makers, pink from the sun, dressed in shorts and T-shirts and wearing caps with *Rio!* emblazoned on them.

'Can we help you?' Quinn says, standing up and dropping the hairbrush on the desk.

'Yes, we read your brochure at our hotel, and it says you do caving trips?'

Katrina realises they are English; and now that the man has spoken, she has the feeling that she knows him from somewhere. He glances over at her, and she thinks she sees a flicker of recognition in his eyes, too, but then it is gone.

'We do indeed do caving trips,' Quinn says. 'We cater for all levels of experience and all types of caving adventures. Was there any particular cave system you wanted to explore?'

The man takes hold of the woman's hand, and Katrina feels a sharp pang of jealousy shoot through her stomach. She guesses they are newlyweds, the way they are standing so close and keep glancing at each other.

'My wife and I are both experienced cavers. We were particularly interested in exploring the Cueva Del Guácharo system; we've heard a lot about it.'

Quinn looks at them suspiciously, as if to say, *This is a joke, right? You know about the oilbirds, don't you?*

'Cueva Del Guácharo is a fascinating system of caves, all right. You do know about the oilbirds, don't you? They leave an awful, stinky mess you have to crawl through to get to the interesting sections.'

Katrina turns away, hiding her smile. She knows Quinn will do anything not to have to go down there again. As she looks out of the window, she sees a man climbing out of a red sports car. It's Ben Stahl, and he is talking to Jay and shaking his hand.

*What's he doing here again?*

'Well, if you're prepared for the mess and the stink, I'd better introduce you to our expert on caving,' Quinn is saying, leading them outside.

The Englishman glances towards Katrina again, that flicker of recognition in his eyes, and Katrina is positive they have met before. She follows them outside, the bright sunlight making her squint. She slips on her sunglasses as Stahl turns and notices her.

'Hey, how are you doing?' He walks towards her, passing Quinn and the English couple. 'You know, I feel like a jerk. You've been through such a frightening experience, and I never thought to properly ask you how you were. I mean, you could have been suffering from some kinda delayed shock or something. I just had to come back and see how you are.'

'Oh, you did more than enough this morning,' Katrina says. 'You got my rucksack back, you gave me a lift into work, what else could you have done?'

Stahl grins that Kodak smile of his. 'I could have — I should have — done lots more. I should have explained what happened, to your boss. I should have checked you were okay before I left you.'

Katrina's not so sure. She's not even sure that Stahl believes what he is saying, and is starting to get the feeling that the American simply wanted an excuse to come back. But why? Is he one of those guys who, as Quinn seems to think, has the hots for her?

Looking at him now, Katrina can't help but think that she isn't his type. But if that is true, what is he doing here? She simply cannot believe he is motivated by concern for her wellbeing.

Just at that moment, Jay is walking past them, talking to the English couple about all the activities they provide. The man suddenly swings around and points at Katrina.

'Hey! Now I know where I've seen you before,' he says. 'Twenty seconds to freefall, right?'

Feeling embarrassed and self-conscious, Katrina remembers where she recognises him from, too. She can't recall his name, but knows he used to be one of her skydiving pupils.

Jay and the American look from the

English couple and then at Katrina, and back again. In any other circumstance, Katrina might have found it funny, watching them turn their heads in synchronisation, as though they are following a tennis match. But instead, the young woman is filled with dread as she realises her secret is about to be exposed to Jay, and he will recognise that she has not been telling him everything.

'What do you mean, 'Twenty seconds to freefall'?' Jay says.

'It was her catchphrase,' the English man replies, looking at Katrina and smiling. 'About two, maybe three years ago now, I was into any kind of sports that had an element of danger about them. I was single at the time,' he glances at his new wife, and his smile grows bigger, 'and I wanted to push myself to the limits, see how far I could go. I decided skydiving would be a perfect sport, and started taking lessons. She was my teacher.'

Katrina wishes the ground would open up and swallow her whole. Jay turns and looks at her, his eyebrows raised in surprise. She can see he wants to ask her about all of this, but she glances down at the ground before he can say anything.

'That was all a long time ago,' she mutters.

The Englishman laughs. 'Don't tell me you've stopped teaching skydiving. You were great.'

'And, tell me more about this catchphrase of hers,' Jay says.

Katrina looks up and sees Jay staring intently at the young man, who is grinning back at him. Stahl is staring at the man too, but he is strangely quiet.

'She used to shout it every time we were about to leave the aeroplane. Other instructors would shout stuff about checking our harnesses, or asking us if we were ready. But not this lady. She always used to shout, 'Twenty seconds to freefall!', and we knew we had to be ready. One last chance to check our harnesses were buckled on, and then start queuing at the exit.'

'Wow.' Jay looks back at Katrina. 'This is fascinating stuff. There's so much about you I don't know, Katrina.'

'There's nothing to know,' Katrina snaps. 'I taught skydiving for a few years and then I stopped. That's all there is to it.'

The Englishman takes a step back and raises his hands in apology. 'Hey, I'm sorry, I didn't mean to upset anybody, you know.'

'It's okay.' Katrina, head down, marches past everybody and off towards the car park exit. She can't stay here any longer; she feels she just has to get away, as far away as she can.

As she walks, she tells herself not to look back, not to let them see how upset she is. She feels foolish now, on top of being angry, embarrassed and miserable, but she knows all she can do is keep walking. It's too late to turn around and apologise for her behaviour — far too late to explain to Jay what happened to her, and how the past shackles her present, and keeps her from starting afresh.

Katrina wonders if she will even be able to go back to work again tomorrow. Jay had begun to trust her more and more, even offering to start the process of teaching her how to skydive, when all along she was living a lie in front of him. How could he ever forgive her?

She hears a car pull up beside her, and a voice say, 'Hey.'

Her heart seems to literally miss a beat, and her stomach flips over, like a giddy schoolgirl on a first date. *It's him!* she thinks. *Jay has seen how upset I am, and come to find me, and tell me he forgives me, that everything is going to be fine. Maybe, just maybe, he does like me. Maybe there can be a future for me, for us, after all.*

She stops and turns, and the smile slowly dies on her face. Ben Stahl is sitting in his red Corvette, grinning up at her.

'You okay? You look like you need a lift back home.' He leans across the passenger seat and opens the door for her. 'Jump in. I'll have you back at your apartment in no time.'

'Oh, no, that's all right, I can catch the bus.'

'Uh-uh.' Stahl wags a finger at her, as though she is a naughty schoolgirl. 'I ain't leaving here until you're in this car. Come on, you'll be doing me a favour. I'll feel like a million bucks again, and it's not often a guy gets to feel like that twice in one day.'

Katrina sighs, and smiles a little. The car ride down here was fun this morning, and maybe a ride back will help lift her mood a little.

'Okay, you're on.' She climbs in the car and shuts the door. 'Home, Jeeves, and don't spare the horses.'

Stahl laughs, and guns the engine as he pulls out into traffic.

* * *

From further down the street, Jay watches as Katrina climbs into the American's car, and they drive off together. It isn't good customer relations to be leaving two prospective clients, but when he had seen the American jump in his flashy sports car and follow Katrina, he had felt as though his heart was being ripped from his chest.

Then Quinn had given him a look, one that brooked no argument, and distinctly said, *Follow them!*

Whilst she had ushered the English couple back into the office, reminding them how filthy and unpleasant oilbirds can be, Jay had run after Katrina.

Now here he is, standing alone and miserable, watching the red sports car disappear through town. A red sports car that Katrina seemed more than happy to climb into.

Again, Jay is sure he has seen the American before today, but can't think where.

Jay turns, head down, and starts walking back to his office. He doesn't notice the car with the shaven-headed man in it, following the American's Corvette.

* * *

Ben Stahl is happier than he has been ever since he arrived in Rio. He's back in his Corvette with a beautiful girl, and this time he can see her curves, and they're nice curves too. But that's not what is making him so happy.

No, the real reason for the big grin on his face is that he finally knows where the USB stick is. He realised where it was when he slipped her apartment keys back into her handbag, the realisation almost making him laugh out loud. He's going to have some fun tonight with this little lady, and at the end of it he will have the USB stick, too.

And tomorrow he will be on a flight back to the USA and a big, fat payday.

# 15

'He wants to take me out to dinner!' Katrina whispers into her mobile. She glances behind her, at the closed bedroom door. Stahl is in the living area, and she doesn't want him to hear her talking. She told him she was going into the bedroom to freshen up.

'I don't know, hun, do you think that's a good idea?' Quinn says, on the other end of the phone.

'You've been the one telling me I need to get out more, and find myself a guy!'

'But not just any guy who drives up and offers you a night out.'

'Maybe he's got the hots for me. You said there are lots of them around. What did you say? Oh yeah, I'm so hot you get the sweats sitting next to me, right?'

'But you hardly know him, babe. All

right, he's got a flash car, and an even flashier grin, but that don't mean anything. You really think he's your type?'

Katrina sighs, well aware that Quinn will have heard that sigh, and interpreted significant meaning from it. 'No, I don't, and I'm not totally convinced I'm his type, either.'

'Well, there you go, hun. Don't go out with him. Just say no.'

'I've tried saying no, several times already, but he's very persistent.'

There's a silence on the other end for a moment, and then Quinn says, 'Tell you what, weren't the two of us meant to be having a girly night out tonight?'

Katrina glances at the bedroom door again, aware of how long she is taking. 'I've tried telling him that, too. He says I can have a girls' night out anytime I want, but he's not going to be here for much longer. Says all he wants is a meal and a drink with a beautiful girl, something to remember Rio by when he's back in the States.'

'Yeeurgh! This guy's got a cheesy routine in chat-up lines, ain't he?'

'Yeah, he's not the most subtle man I've ever met, even for an American. What am I going to do, Quinn? He's here right now, in my apartment, and I just can't get rid of him.'

'Tell you what. Say yes to him, then tell me where you're going. I'll drag Enrique away from his protester friends and we'll turn up too. Just by accident, like, know what I mean?'

'Quinn, I love you. Seriously, I do.'

'Yeah, well, it's about time I got to spend some time with my man. Seems like he's starting to take all this environmental protest jive a bit too seriously. I mean, you know, I realise the earth's our friend an' all, and needs some help right now, but my man's gotta realise I have a need for him too. A real urgent kind of need, if you know what I'm saying.'

Katrina smiles. 'I'll see you later. Oh, wait! Quinn, was Jay very mad at me for walking off like that?'

'He ain't a happy bunny right now, hun. He ain't happy at all.'

With that, Quinn breaks the connection. Katrina switches off her mobile and slips it back in her pocket. She stays sitting on the bed, looking at the closed bedroom door. Atticus is prowling around her feet, purring loudly, his tail flicking between her ankles.

Stahl has been good to her, but she can't help feeling a little uneasy in his presence sometimes. Even Atticus doesn't seem to like him, preferring to keep his distance from the American. Katrina can't quite pin down what it is about Stahl that she doesn't like. His cheesy grin and outdated fashion sense don't endear him to her, nor does his corny way of talking. But there's something else — an indefinable aura he has, his posture and body language. Katrina has an uneasy sense that the American might not be quite as nice a person as he presents himself to be.

Still, she feels better knowing that if she goes out with him tonight, Quinn and Enrique will be there too.

And she feels bad about walking out on Jay like that. After all, he's been good to her, too. He took her on as a dive leader when he really didn't know all that much about her; and, along with Quinn, he's looked after her while she found her feet in Rio.

*He's a good man*, she thinks. *Cute, too.*

More than that, they seem to be drawing closer to each other. Katrina never set out to become close to another man. Up until last night, she had no intention of becoming involved with anyone ever again. But Jay is different and, despite the false starts they have had, Katrina is wondering if this might be the beginning of a new chapter in her life.

She decides, there and then, that tomorrow she will go and explain everything to him. She will tell him all about Pete, and the dreadful day of his accident, and hope that he will understand. Katrina knows this could be a fresh start for her, and she has to seize the opportunity before Jay cools off and starts looking elsewhere for a girlfriend. Still, Katrina feels the dark shadow of her fiancé's tragic accident looming over her; but maybe telling Jay about Pete will help her throw off the shackles of the past.

Katrina slips her shoes off and kicks them under the bed. She is surprised to feel them encounter some resistance, and hear them brush up against something. Ever since moving into the apartment, Katrina has kept the underside of the bed clear. It's a habit she has always had, hating clutter of any kind.

But now there appears to be something under there. She has no memory of putting anything under the bed, and cannot think what it might be. She is about to bend down and look under the bed when she flinches, as Stahl pounds on the bedroom door.

'Hey, come on, Katrina, how long can it take a girl to freshen up?'

Katrina stands up. 'Just a minute! Almost done.'

She opens her wardrobe and chooses

a dress. She pulls off her work clothes, sprays on some body freshener, and slips into the dress. 'Where do you want to go tonight, anyway?' she shouts, brushing her hair.

'I know a place down by the seafront, got great views of Sugarloaf, and they make the best caipirinha in Rio.'

'Sounds great. What's it called?'

'Porcâo Rio's. You'll love it. Now come on, what's taking you so long?'

'Almost ready!' Katrina grabs her mobile and quickly texts the name of the restaurant to Quinn. She only hopes she will be as good as her word, and turn up with Enrique.

She doesn't really fancy spending the evening alone with Ben Stahl.

* * *

Katrina has to admit, Stahl is right. The restaurant does indeed have fantastic views across the harbour and, in the distance, Sugarloaf Mountain. The restaurant itself is a delight, too: elegant and refined, whereas the Baronetti is garish and loud, Porcâo Rio's exudes calm and sophistication. Bow-tied waiters slip elegantly between tables, and the enormous buffet is filled with barbequed beef, chicken and pork, salads and sushi.

They have a table by a large open window, giving them the atmosphere of the restaurant with the views and the gentle breeze of outside. Stahl consumes caipirinha after caipirinha, constantly exhorting Katrina to match him drink for drink. The more alcohol he downs, the louder he gets, until couples at other tables begin casting pointed looks their way. Every now and then, Katrina slips a glance at her watch, wondering when Quinn and Enrique will turn up.

The American is boring and self-obsessed. Despite her earlier misgivings, part of her had thought the date might turn out to be fun, but now she can't wait to get away. It doesn't help her mood that she can't stop thinking about Jay, wondering what he is doing, and wishing it was him sitting across the table from her instead of Stahl.

Katrina smiles thinly as Stahl tells her another in a seemingly endless stream of awful jokes. He then pounds the table with the flat of his hand, and brays with laughter. To Katrina, the sound of his laughter is like fingernails being scraped down a blackboard. The only thing that stops her walking out on him is her uncertainty about his response. Katrina is beginning to get the feeling that Stahl does not like it when people refuse him something. She can't help but wonder what kind of reaction she would get if she stood up and attempted to leave.

Just as she feels she can take no more, that she will simply have to stand up and make her excuses, no matter what the consequences, she sees something which takes her mind completely off Stahl for a moment.

Walking past the restaurant, almost silhouetted against the evening sun reflected off the sea, Katrina sees Jay.

Her tummy performs a perfect little somersault, and her instinct is to cry out and attract his attention. A torrent of thoughts rushes through her mind: how she wants to apologise for her behaviour earlier; how she wants to tell him of her dread of flying, and the loss of her one, true love.

She almost stands up and calls his name, when she sees he is with another woman. She is tall and slender, and very beautiful. And they are laughing together as they walk. Katrina's heart drops to her stomach, and she feels sick with despair. What has she been thinking? How could she allow herself to believe that she and Jay might have a mutual attraction, that they might even have the beginnings of a future together? She realises now, with a crushing finality, that she has been acting like a besotted teenager with a stupid schoolgirl crush on someone who hardly even knows she exists. Her idea that, once she explains everything to Jay about Pete's accident, Jay will fall into her arms declaring his undying love for her, suddenly seems ridiculous and silly.

*What on earth would Jay ever see in me?* she thinks. *I should move on, leave Rio, go travelling again. There's nothing to keep me here.*

'What's wrong?' Stahl says, interrupting Katrina's thoughts. 'Have you even listened to a thing I've said just now?'

'Sorry,' Katrina mutters, as Jay and the woman disappear from her line of sight. 'I just thought I saw someone I knew, that's all.'

Stahl grunts, downs another drink, and wipes his mouth with the back of his hand. 'Yeah, well, we have a good table here for sightseeing, that's why I chose it.'

'What do you mean?'

Stahl leans forward, emphasising his words by pointing at her. 'You know, everything I've told you so far tonight has been a complete fabrication. But you're a smart girl, Katrina, and I want to be honest with you.'

Katrina looks at him, waiting, wondering what's coming next.

'Katrina, I work for the CIA, and I'm here in Rio on an important mission.'

'Really?' Katrina is not sure what to think here. Stahl seemed a nice man when she first met him this morning, and he retrieved her rucksack from the muggers. But the more she spends time with him this evening, the less she likes him. He is self-obsessed and arrogant.

'Yeah, really. I shouldn't be telling you this, but you're an intelligent woman, Katrina, and I can see that I can trust you. I'm here on the trail of an Iranian hitman.'

Katrina can't help but gasp. 'Is his name Kubaschi?'

Now it is Stahl's turn to look startled. 'That's right. How do you know that?'

'There was an old man, an English scientist, who died last night. He had a heart attack and fell into my arms. The police say that he mentioned Kubaschi's name just before he died.'

Stahl looks thoughtful. Katrina wonders if she should tell him the whole story. Maybe the reason Lowenstein was in Rio is part of why Stahl is here too. But before she gets the chance to do that, Stahl is talking again.

'Kubaschi's a nasty piece of work, a real slimeball. He's murdered more people than you've ever met, and in more gruesome, disgusting ways than you can imagine. And he likes to take his time about it, too.'

'But why is he here in Rio?'

'That's what I'm here to find out, baby. Listen, I shouldn't have told you any of this. I can see I've put the wind up you, but you don't have to worry. The reason I got us this table with a view up and down the street is so I can keep a lookout for him. Everywhere I go, I make sure I'm in a position to be able to see what's going on, who's coming and going.' Stahl takes her hand in his, and Katrina inwardly cringes. 'Don't worry, you're safe with me. But do me a favour, huh? Keep a lookout for a swarthy, shaven-headed guy. That's Kubaschi, and if you see him, just give me a call, okay?'

'Okay.' Katrina pulls her hand away and takes a sip of her drink. Stahl is soon off again, regaling her with more stories about himself.

Just as Katrina is resigning herself to having to spend the rest of the evening with Stahl, she sees Quinn, with Enrique right behind her, entering the restaurant. She waves at them, resisting the urge to let her smile grow too big, to let her relief be too obvious.

'Quinn! What a surprise! What are you doing here?'

Quinn strides over and stands by their table, towering over the two of them. 'Hey, hun, just out on a date with my man. What say we make it a double?'

'Hi, Katrina,' Enrique says, ambling over with a big, easy grin on his face, lifting a hand in greeting.

Stahl glares at them both. 'Actually, this is a private party.'

'Don't be like that,' Katrina says. 'These are my friends, of course they can join us.'

Quinn looks around, catching the eye of a passing waiter. 'Hey, can we have another two chairs here?'

The waiter nods and rushes off. The restaurant is crowded, and Katrina doubts he will find any free chairs.

Stahl is frowning, and he is gripping the edges of the table, his knuckles turning white with the exertion. 'This table's far too small for four of us,' he says.

Quinn laughs. 'Don't worry about it, brother, we all friends here — or at least we soon will be.'

The waiter returns, carrying two chairs. Quinn and Enrique sit down. Suddenly the table for two looks very crowded.

'Hey, my man,' Enrique says, holding out a hand for Stahl to high five. 'How's it going?'

Stahl regards the offered hand as though it is crawling with the bubonic plague. 'Do I know you?'

Enrique just grins at him, his hand still raised, waiting for that high five.

Quinn laughs. 'I doubt it, but that don't matter to my man. Until he decides otherwise, everybody is a friend to Enrique, whether he knows you or not.'

Enrique, seeing that Stahl has no intention of high-fiving him, claps him on the shoulder instead. 'I like your style, you know? You're too cool for school, Moses, I can see that.'

The American recoils from the slap on the shoulder and stares at Enrique as though he is speaking gibberish. Enrique smiles right back at him.

Katrina is so happy and relieved to see her friends, her hands are trembling. She stuffs them under her thighs, sitting on them to stop the shakes.

A waiter arrives and begins laying out cutlery for the new arrivals. They are squashed together round the small table, but the restaurant is crowded and all the other tables are occupied.

'Hey, are we eatin'?' Enrique eyes Katrina's barbecued chicken with undisguised lust.

'Yeah, we're eatin' all right.' Quinn

stares hard at the waiter. 'I'll have the pork, and my man'll have a barbecued chicken.'

'Would that be chicken wings, sir?'

'Don't bother 'bout none o' that fancy stuff, just barbecue me a whole chicken, my man,' says Enrique. 'I've got a terrible hunger on me tonight.'

Katrina claps a hand over her mouth to keep from laughing out loud. She knows that they are putting on a show, exaggerating their personalities, and playing up to Stahl for her benefit. And she loves them dearly for it.

'So, what's fresh with the news then, Lewis?' Enrique reaches out and lightly punches Stahl on the arm.

The American leaps to his feet, knocking over his chair, and rattling the cutlery on the table. Some of the other customers turn and look at the disturbance.

'Don't you dare lay another finger on me!' Stahl, his jaw clenched, and a pulse visibly throbbing in his neck, points at Enrique. He turns his head and looks at Katrina. 'We're leaving now.'

Katrina shakes her head. 'No.'

'What did you say?' Stahl lowers his hand, and Katrina sees him make a fist.

'I said, no.' Katrina's voice is calm, but inside she is almost as scared as when she saw the shark. Had that been just this morning? To Katrina, it seems like a week ago. 'I'm staying here with my friends.'

Stahl's face is flushed with rage. Now she can see the consequences of refusing him. He is like a spoiled child who, for the first time in his life, has not got his own way. Katrina is afraid of what he might do next. She has visions of him, like a little boy refused a treat, rushing at them with his fists flying. But this image, she realises with frightening certainty, belittles him, and diminishes his power, and the terrible things he might well be capable of.

Stahl, true to Katrina's prediction, takes a step toward her, his hands by his sides, clenching and unclenching.

Enrique stands up. He is tall and muscular, and towers over the American.

'Hey, my man, slow down, take it easy.'

Stahl glowers up at Enrique. 'I could snap your neck like a piece of balsa wood if I wanted to.'

Enrique extends his hands out in an open invitation. 'Let's do it, man.'

Katrina is aware that the whole restaurant has fallen silent now — that all eyes are upon them, waiting to see how this plays out.

Stahl stares at Enrique for a few seconds longer, as though he is weighing up his options. Then, without another word, he spins round and stalks out of the restaurant.

'Phew!' Quinn whistles. 'Who put a firecracker up his ass?'

Katrina feels all the energy draining out of her, as though she had been filled to bursting with water, and somebody pulled the plug out. 'Guys, thank you ever so much. I owe you both big time.'

Enrique bends down and plants the lightest of kisses on Katrina's cheek. 'You owe us nothin', Kat. You one special lady, an' you deserve better than the likes of him. If he ever bothers you again, just let me know, an' I'll deal with him.'

On impulse, Katrina stands up and wraps her arms around Enrique, holding him tight.

'Hey, put my man down!' Quinn shouts.

Enrique waves her over, and so she stands up and joins them. They have a group hug in the middle of Porcâo Rio's, and all the other diners start applauding.

# 16

They start the walk back to Katrina's apartment together, arm-in-arm, with Katrina in the middle, chatting and laughing. Quinn tells them how she managed to persuade the English couple not to go down Cueva Del Guácharo, that the oilbirds are just too filthy and disgusting, and that the caverns aren't worth it. 'There's no way I was going down there again.' But her plan backfired, and Quinn failed to persuade the couple to book another trip instead, so they left without spending any money. 'Jay didn't speak to me for the rest of the afternoon!' Quinn says.

'Well, he was probably already mad at me for walking out on him,' Katrina says. 'And I don't blame him. First thing tomorrow, I'm going to apologise, and tell him everything. He deserves an explanation.'

'And then maybe you two can come back to Porcâo Rio's tomorrow night and do some celebrating, right, hun?'

Katrina stops, pulling the other two to a dead halt. 'That reminds me, I still haven't given you two a piece of my mind for that blatant stunt you pulled last night.'

Quinn steps back, a look of comical bewilderment on her face. 'What you talkin' about, hun?'

Katrina looks from her to Enrique, who suddenly turns away with an, 'Excuse me!' and starts coughing. But his shoulders are shaking suspiciously, like he is trying to control a fit of laughter.

'You know exactly what I'm talking about,' Katrina says, staring at Quinn. 'Last night at Baronetti's, telling me Enrique was bringing a friend with him, some hot guy who would be perfect for me, when all the time it was Jay!'

'What's wrong with that?' Quinn asks, holding out her arms. 'Jay is pretty damn hot, right?'

'Watch your mouth, girl,' Enrique gasps, between bursts of laughter.

A thought surfaces in Katrina's mind. They were in Baronetti's bar just last night. It seems an age ago now, as though it happened in another life time. But it didn't happen a lifetime ago; only last night she saw Oliver Lowenstein collapse, and then she had spent the rest of the night talking with Jay, who had arrived with Enrique.

Suddenly it hits Katrina that she hasn't been to bed in over thirty-six hours. 'Oh my god!' With the realisation of how long she has been awake, a wave of tiredness washes over her. Katrina stumbles slightly, and Quinn grabs her by the arm.

'What? What's wrong, babe? You look ill. Did you eat something bad?'

'No, I'm fine,' Katrina says, her voice starting to slur. She can't believe how quickly her energy levels are plummeting. 'You know what? I just want to go home, to bed.' She yawns a huge, mouth painfully wide open, long, aching yawn.

The kind that says, if I don't get to bed now, I'm just going to drop to the floor and sleep where I land.

'Did you get any sleep last night?' Quinn says, her eyebrows arched quizzically.

Katrina shakes her head, and it seems as though she now has a floppy doll's head on a body full of cotton-wool stuffing. She fuzzily wonders if she can even make it back to her apartment. Her legs have suddenly lost the power to keep her upright, never mind the ability to walk. She has obviously been running on adrenaline and coffee all day, but now the lack of sleep has caught up with her big-time.

Enrique puts a strong arm around her and supports her weight. 'Come on, let's get you back.'

By the time they arrive at Katrina's apartment the night is drawing in and the city is coming alive. Screams of laughter echo down the cobbled streets, and the clubs and bars illuminate the alleys with their neon glow. Katrina is aware of the pounding disco beats emanating from the clubs, but knows that once she collapses on her bed, nothing will rouse her.

'Almost there,' Enrique is saying as they enter the building's lobby.

'Katrina!'

Katrina looks up, trying to focus on the person speaking to her. The voice sounds very familiar, but she can't quite get a hang on who it is.

'Katrina, what's wrong with you? Are you drunk?'

'No, she ain't drunk, just dog-tired is all,' Quinn says.

*Who are you?* Katrina wonders. *Why are you so interested in me, and how come Quinn knows you?*

Making a supreme effort, using all the willpower she has left, Katrina lifts her head, which now feels so heavy she is convinced it has been filled with concrete, and focuses on the person in front of her. 'Jay?' she mumbles. 'Wataryoodoo-ineer?'

'I was looking for you,' Jay says.

Katrina wants to tell him that she saw him earlier — she saw him with the young woman, the *beautiful* young woman, and how she might be beautiful but she's not right for him, no, not in a million years . . .

The next thing she is aware of, she is being carried upstairs and into her apartment, and then she is falling mercifully into a deep, wonderful sleep.

* * *

'Go away,' she mumbles, and turns over.

Right at this moment in time, Katrina's bed is the most delicious, wonderful place to be in the whole, wide world. She doubts that even an earthquake could shift her from under her sheets. How could she have lasted for so many hours without sleep?

Katrina allows herself to be pulled under once more, her thoughts disappearing into nothingness; promising herself, with the last of her conscious thought, to allow nothing and no one to drag her awake until she is ready.

But then, only a moment later, she is sleepily stirring again, turning over onto her opposite side, growing annoyed that some irritant is keeping her from going fast asleep. 'Go away,' she mumbles again. 'Leave me alone.'

Just as she is drifting away again, the pounding on her door catches her before she is gone completely, and wakens her a little more.

Katrina paws at her bedside clock, trying to wrap her fingers around the black cube so that she can pick it up and look at the time. But her hand and arm seem unable to obey her mind, and her hand misses the clock a couple of times, then finally bashes into it and knocks it on the floor.

Lying face-down on the bed, her arm hanging over the side, she pats the floor, trying to find the clock. Under the bed her fingers encounter an object, something that feels like it might be wrapped in plastic. This brings back a vague memory of realising there is something under her bed, but not knowing what.

*In the morning*, she thinks. *I'll have a look in the morning*.

She gives up searching for the clock and is about to turn over and drift off once more, when whoever is outside her apartment pounds on the door again.

Katrina is reluctantly starting to wake up more now. She finds the clock and lifts it up to her face, examining the digital display with bleary eyes.

1:05

Katrina has no idea what time she got back, or how long she has been asleep, but she knows it can't have been long. And now somebody has the nerve to wake her up by knocking on her door!

She half climbs, half falls out of bed, and stumbles through her lounge. With her lolloping gait and hair sticking out in wild tangles, she is pretty sure that she looks like a B-movie zombie, and that when she opens her door the person on the other side will run screaming into the night.

That would be good. At least she could go back to bed.

But when she finally gets enough coordination in her hands to unlock her door and open it, it is Katrina who catches her breath, and has to stifle the instinct to turn and run.

'Hey, listen, I'm sorry if I got you up,' Stahl says, smiling that smile that now looks more like a shark's grin than before. 'But I just had to come and apologise for earlier. I was out of order.'

Katrina pushes hair out of her face, feeling embarrassed and vulnerable in nothing but her oversized T-shirt. She pulls it down a little lower over her thighs. 'There's no need to apologise.'

'Uh, I think there is. I was a jerk, and if that friend of yours had floored me, I would have deserved it.' Stahl takes a step forward, and then another, and before Katrina realises it he is in the room and has shut the door behind him. 'You know, sometimes I just get uptight around other people, especially people I don't know.'

'It's okay, really. It's fine.'

'No, it's not.' Stahl holds his hands in the air and takes another step closer. 'I admit it, I'm a loser. I should know better, I know I should.'

'It's nice of you to come around and apologise,' Katrina says, trying to keep her voice calm and level, not wanting to let him know how scared she is starting to get. 'But I'm seriously tired, and I just need to go back to bed.'

'Yeah, bed. Now that sounds nice. How about if I keep you company, you know, help you get to sleep?'

'No, that's not necessary.'

Stahl steps closer. 'I could give you a massage, help you relax.'

'You need to go now,' Katrina says, putting everything in to making her voice commanding, firm. She can hear excited voices from outside, the music pounding from the night clubs, and she wonders if anyone will hear her scream. And even if they do, will they just think it's someone else having a good time, yelling with joy, rather than fear?

Looking into Stahl's eyes, she can see he is thinking similar things. He knows he is safe in here for the moment. He has plenty of time. He can do whatever he wants with her, and nobody will come to her rescue.

Not unless she gets to her bedroom window, and leans outside and screams for help.

Katrina turns and bolts for the bedroom. She barrels through her bedroom door, scrambling over her bed and snatching up the bedside clock as she goes. Her plan is to throw it at the window, smash the glass and scream blue murder.

But Stahl is right behind her. She can hear him grunt as he leaps over her bed. She raises her hand, ready to hurl the clock at the window pane with all her strength, when Stahl's hand closes around her wrist and he yanks her back, onto the bed. Katrina yells in pain; her shoulder is on fire. It feels like he has twisted her arm out of its socket, but she still manages to hold onto the clock. Stahl straddles her and sits on her thighs. He is breathing heavily and his face is tight with rage and lust.

'Let me go!' Katrina screams.

Stahl says nothing, his breathing now fast and shallow. He unbuckles his belt, and fumbles with the zip on his trousers.

Katrina, ignoring the hot, searing pain in her shoulder, brings her hand up in a wide arc, and smashes the bedside clock into the side of Stahl's head. Shards of black plastic go flying, and the impact knocks him sideways. Not enough to get him off her, but it distracts him for a moment. Katrina uses that second to grab him between the legs and squeeze hard. He screams in agony, and she pushes him onto the floor.

She rolls off the bed and scrabbles for the door on her hands and knees. Stahl is roaring at her like a wounded animal. Katrina knows she has done nothing to stop him, and only succeeded in making him angry. Her only chance now is to get out of the apartment, downstairs and outside where she will be safe in the crowds, amongst people.

She reaches the bedroom door and stands up, fumbling with the door handle.

Stahl slams into her from behind and throws her to the floor, knocking the breath from her lungs. He stands over her, his hands clenching and unclenching.

'Get up,' he growls.

Katrina sits up, watching him all the time. Stahl lunges down and grabs her by the hair, hauling her over to the bed. He slams her back down on the mattress, then grips her by her hair.

'This time you're gonna be a good little girl,' he says, his voice husky, barely more than a whisper. 'And give me what I came here for.'

Katrina grips the bed sheets, screwing them up between her fingers.

*No*, she promises herself, the resolve to continue fighting back growing within her. *I won't give you anything at all*.

# 17

Jay, Quinn and Enrique thread their way through the crowded streets, heading home. Jay managed to get a few hours' worth of sleep after work, but not enough to make up for last night. It's been a busy day, with the excitement of the shark encounter, and then the revelation that Katrina is an accomplished skydiver, and he can feel the tiredness catching up with him again.

Still, he hadn't expected Katrina to be so flaked out when he met her at her apartment. He had seen her earlier in the evening, at Porcâo Rio's, with Ben Stahl. After Katrina had inexplicably walked out on them, and Quinn had lost them some custom because of her hatred of oilbird guano, Jay had got so angry he had left for home too. When the Englishman had revealed her talents for skydiving, before Katrina drove off in Stahl's sports car, Jay had felt as though the rug had been pulled from beneath him. He knew there must be more to the story than that, but at that point he had been too angry to care. When he had arrived home he had called an old girlfriend, to see if she wanted to hook up again and go out on a date.

It had seemed like a good idea at the time. Jay had begun to think he and Katrina were drawing closer, that she was starting to lower her defences, and maybe let him in a little. Jay has never perceived himself as somebody who is shy, and he has always had his fair share of girlfriends.

But Katrina is different. With her he loses all the confidence and sure-footedness that he usually has when dealing with the opposite sex. Is it the aura of mystery that she has about her? After all, he knows so little about her life before she turned up in Rio, and she has always met his questions with vague generalisations or changes of subject.

But no, there's something else about her — something indefinable that draws him in and seems to promise that she is the one. She is the girl he can see himself settling down with, spending the rest of his life with.

Which is ridiculous, when he stops to think about how little he knows about her.

But earlier today, when they were hauling the scuba gear into the shed, and Quinn was being paraded around the car park by the Chileans, Jay sensed they had made a connection. He could tell that Katrina felt the same way too.

And then the English couple and Stahl had turned up, and between them they ruined everything.

So Jay had called up an ex, they had headed out on the town, and for a while he had been having fun. But as soon as he glimpsed Katrina in the restaurant with Stahl, the evening turned sour. Not long after that he decided to make his excuses and head for home. He knew he wouldn't be seeing that particular ex anytime again; she had not been pleased at all when they said goodbye.

On his way back home, Jay had changed his mind and headed over to Katrina's apartment, with the aim of meeting her when she got back and having a sit-down and a talk. But seeing Quinn and Enrique helping a barely conscious Katrina inside had put paid to that idea.

Quinn had put Katrina to bed whilst Jay and Enrique sat in the living area. Enrique had filled him in with what had happened earlier in the evening. Jay doesn't like the sound of Stahl at all, and he wonders at his motives for paying Katrina so much attention. Quinn thinks he's just a typical American blowhard: big flashy car, even flashier grin, thinks he can strut up and down and do whatever he pleases, take whatever he wants.

'Needs bringing down a peg or two,' she said earlier, and then looked adoringly at Enrique. 'Which is just what my man did tonight.'

Jay's not so sure, though. He doesn't think they have seen the last of Ben Stahl. Besides which, he has finally remembered where he has seen the American before.

It was the previous night, at Baronetti's. Jay and Enrique had just arrived, pushing their way through the crowded club, and Jay was wondering why there was no music playing. By that time of night the DJ usually had the beats pounding out at top volume, but when they walked through the doors, all they could hear was the chatter of the crowd.

Jay soon realised what the problem was when he saw the old man laid out on the table. That was when he had noticed Stahl. For a moment it had appeared to Jay as though the American was rifling through the old man's pockets. Then the crowd closed in around the man on the table and Jay had lost sight of him.

Jay had reached out and stopped someone walking past. 'What's happening?'

'Old dude pushed his way into the club and collapsed in some girl's arms. What a way to go, huh?'

Jay had pushed his way through the people surrounding the old man, curious to see the American again. But Stahl had gone, and soon after that the paramedics arrived, and Jay had not given him another thought.

But now, Jay finds he can think of nothing else but Ben Stahl.

'Wait up, guys,' Jay says. 'I think I'm going to head back to Katrina's apartment.'

'I know you wanna have a heart-to-heart with Katrina, but now's not the time, outback guy,' Quinn says.

'It's not that.' Jay pauses, trying to pull his thoughts together. 'I've just got a bad feeling about this Stahl guy. I'd like to go back and just check that Katrina's okay, that's all.'

'You want me to come, too?' Enrique says.

'No, you two have done more than enough already. I can handle this.' He looks at Quinn. 'I'll see you in the morning. And hey, no more scaring customers away with all your crazy talk about oilbirds, okay?'

'Okay, boss.' Quinn smiles and salutes.

Jay turns and heads back into the crowds, his pace quickening as he thinks about Ben Stahl.

* * *

Stahl is pulling Katrina's hair so tight her head is bent back, the tendons in her neck feeling like they might snap. He grunts as he climbs up on the bed with her, his face contorted in an angry rage.

'You've got something I want, and I'm gonna get it,' he growls. 'But we have plenty of time for a little fun before then.'

Katrina lets go of the bed sheets, her hands flying to his face, and digs her nails into the flesh. She drags her fingers down, over his forehead and his eyes and into the soft flesh of his cheeks, trying to force her nails deep into that face that she hates so much.

Stahl howls, letting go of her hair, and staggers off the bed. Katrina sits up, surprised at her own ferocity. Still on the bed, Katrina gets onto her feet, squatting to keep her balance. The American is between her and the bedroom door. She has nowhere to go. Stahl begins approaching her, but stops and blinks, and wipes blood from his eyes. Katrina rolls off the opposite side of the bed and slides a drawer out of her bedside cabinet.

She flings the drawer at Stahl, who manages to bat it away, scattering the contents across the floor. She drags a second drawer out, throwing the contents onto the bed and then flinging the drawer at him. Again he bats the missile away.

Katrina grabs her nail scissors from the pile of stuff on the bed and holds them out at arm's length. Not much of a weapon, but the only one she has left.

'Keep away,' she hisses.

Stahl says nothing. He pulls off his jacket and throws it behind him. His T-shirt is pulled tight over his powerful body. Katrina knows she hasn't got much fight left, and he is far stronger than she is. So far she has been lucky, but her luck can't hold, and Stahl doesn't look as though he is about to give up on her any time soon.

The American begins walking around the bed, holding his hands, palms out, in front of him. 'Why don't you put those itty-bitty scissors down? You know they're not going to do you any good. Do you seriously think they can hurt me?'

'Back off!' Katrina lunges with the scissors, even though he is still too far away for her to stab him.

Stahl grins, and he looks even more demonic than ever. 'Put the scissors down. Tell you what — if you give me what I want, we can forego the fun. How about that?'

Katrina backs up against the window. If she turns to open it he will be on her before she knows it, and she doesn't think she has the strength to fight him off again. She thinks about smashing the glass with her elbow or fist, but she's not sure she has the strength to do that either, or how quickly she can manage it.

Someone knocking on Katrina's door distracts Stahl.

He looks back at Katrina. 'Don't say a word, or I will kill you.'

Katrina only hesitates a fraction of a second.

'Help me!' she screams. 'Help me, I'm being attacked!'

Stahl's mouth curls into a sneer as the door begins trembling in its frame, under the onslaught of a series of powerful hits against it. He backs up to the wall, standing beside the open bedroom doorway.

The apartment door flies open and Jay comes staggering through, his momentum carrying him across the living area. He sees Katrina, his eyes widening in shock. Before she has chance to warn him, Stahl steps out from his hiding place beside the bedroom door and slams a fist into Jay's stomach.

Jay doubles over, the breath exploding from him in a 'Whoof!', and Stahl pushes him over. The American raises a foot to kick him, but Jay grabs his ankle as he swings his foot towards his head. Jay yanks his leg and Stahl falls over, landing with a grunt on his back.

As Jay is clambering to his feet, Stahl lashes out with a foot and connects with Jay's stomach again. Jay doubles over once more and collapses to the floor. Stahl jumps up and, before Katrina can think about what she will do next, he has fled the apartment.

Katrina drops the scissors and runs to Jay, bending down beside him. He rolls over onto his side, clutching his stomach and groaning.

'Jay, are you all right?'

'Yeah, I think I'm okay,' Jay gasps. 'He just winded me.'

'But he got you in the stomach twice. Are you sure you're okay?'

'Yeah.' The Australian sits up and looks at Katrina, a worried frown creasing his forehead. 'What about you? Are you hurt? Did he . . . ?'

'No, I'm fine, don't worry.' Katrina suddenly feels extremely self-conscious. Her T-shirt has ridden up her thighs a little, and she pulls it back down again. 'Let me go make myself a little more decent.'

She hurries into the bedroom and pulls on a dressing gown, and then she starts trembling violently, and has to sit down on the bed before she falls down. A few moments later, Jay appears in the doorway. He is still clutching his stomach, but standing up, at least.

'Hey,' he says, coming and sitting down next to her.

He puts an arm around her shoulder and she leans into him, and the next thing she knows, she is crying.

'Sshh, it's okay, he's gone now,' Jay whispers.

'I thought I was going to die,' Katrina manages to say, between sobs. 'I could see it in his eyes. Once he had raped me, he was going to kill me. I know he was.'

'But he didn't do any of that. You fought him off, Katrina.'

Katrina wraps her arms around Jay's torso and holds him tight. 'I can't stay here tonight.'

'Of course not,' Jay says. 'You're coming back to mine.'

Katrina squeezes Jay even tighter. 'Thank you.' She feels calmer now, safe. She might feel like crying again later, but for now the tears are over, and in their place is tiredness.

'Come on, let's get you back.'

Jay helps Katrina to her feet. She tries to clear her mind of what has just happened, concentrating on things that she needs to take with her. She finds her rucksack and drops her handbag into it, and some spare clothes and toiletries. Jay closes her bedroom door and leaves her to get dressed.

Even though she knows he is just next door, Katrina feels vulnerable and alone. As quick as she can she pulls on a fresh top and shorts. Her hands won't stop trembling, and she has to sit down again at one point, when her legs feel like they will give way under her.

Jay knocks on the bedroom door and opens it a crack. 'Are you okay?'

'Come in, I'm fine. A lot better than I would have been if you hadn't turned up.'

Jay opens the door wide. 'I was worried about you.'

Katrina looks up at Jay and smiles. 'That's nice. But why were you worrying about me? Wait a minute! Were you here earlier, when I was completely zonked out?'

Jay sits down next to her. 'Yeah. I was waiting for you.'

'God, I must have looked awful. Did I look as terrible as I felt?'

Jay grins. 'I don't know, but I'm guessing you must have felt pretty bloody awful if that was the case.'

Katrina sighs. 'I must be a proper sight right now.'

'You look just great, like a survivor.'

'Thanks. I think.'

'That guy, Stahl, do you know much about him?'

'No. He said he is in the CIA, but I don't believe him.'

'I don't, either. You know, Katrina, I saw him at the Baronetti the night the old man collapsed and died. When they had laid him out on the table, I saw Stahl standing over him. At first I thought he was trying to help him, but then it looked more like he was rifling through the old man's pockets.'

'What do you think he was after?'

Jay runs his fingers through his hair. 'I don't know.'

'The weird thing is, when Stahl was trying to convince me earlier that he works for the CIA, he said he was on the trail of a hitman called Kubaschi. I had a visit from Detective Benzali yesterday, and he told me that Lowenstein mentioned Kubaschi's name just before he died, as well as saying my name too.'

'Do you have any idea what's going on?'

Katrina shakes her head. 'None at all.

Wait a minute.' She roots through her bag and pulls out a business card. 'I've got Detective Benzali's mobile number here. He told me to call him any time I wanted. I think this might be a good time, don't you?'

'Absolutely. For one thing, you need to report Stahl to the police. There's no knowing what he'll do next.'

Katrina taps in the number, and waits for it to start ringing. She gives Jay a nervous smile, an image of Stahl leaping for her suddenly flashing through her mind, and giving her a shiver.

The mobile starts ringing.

'Can you hear that?' Jay says.

'What?'

'Listen.'

Katrina pulls the phone away from her ear, and then she can hear it too. The muffled sound of a mobile phone, ringing, waiting to be answered. To Katrina it almost sounds as though it is coming from underneath the bed.

Katrina puts her mobile back to her ear, but Benzali has not answered. She hangs up, and the muffled ringing from beneath the bed stops too.

Katrina and Jay look at each other.

'Try again,' Jay whispers.

Katrina redials, and the faint, indistinct ringing starts up again.

Leaving her mobile connected, Katrina places it on the bed. She remembers now — that thing under the bed, when there shouldn't be anything under there. Slowly, feeling as though she is moving through treacle, as though her limbs no longer want to obey her, she gets down onto her knees and lowers her head.

She looks under the bed.

And screams.

Encased in clear, heavy-duty plastic, she can see Benzali's head, his face turned towards her, his lifeless eyes staring back at her.

'Katrina?'

Jay gets down on the floor and looks under the bed as Katrina backs away, unable to tear her eyes away from the dead body.

'Dear God,' Jay whispers.

'It's Detective Benzali. Stahl must have done this; he killed him. He's been here, in my apartment, and murdered Benzali.' Katrina stands up, feeling close to hysteria. She takes a deep breath, struggling to get control of herself. Jay stands up and she grabs hold of him, and they start backing out of the bedroom, Katrina holding onto Jay as though he is a lifeline.

In the living room they pause, and Katrina closes her eyes for a moment, trying to dispel the image of Benzali's face distorted by the clear plastic, staring back at her. But it is no good, and she feels she will carry that image around with her forever.

'We need to get out of here,' Jay says, taking her by the arm and leading her to her front door. 'As soon as we get outside we'll call the police, but I don't think we should hang around here any longer.'

They head for the door when suddenly it slams open and a man steps inside.

Katrina screams again as Jay pushes her behind him. They both instantly recognise the shaven-headed man in the doorway as Kubaschi. And he is pointing a gun at them.

# 18

Katrina is suddenly overcome with a sense of complete calm. As she stands next to Jay, facing the man with a gun pointing at them, she loses all her fear. It is as though she has been pushed to the very limits of what she can take, and then dropped over the edge.

The feeling reminds her of the hours following Pete's death. She remembers thinking then that none of it was real, that she would arrive home that night and find him waiting for her. Losing a loved one in a terrible accident wasn't what happened to people like Katrina. That kind of thing only happened on the news, to other people, to strangers.

Katrina had floated through the rest of the day on a wave of numbness. And of course at the end of the day she hadn't gone home, but had been taken to her parents' house, where she remained for the next six months. She never returned to the house that she shared with Pete, that had been intended as their marital home.

Katrina sold the house and, suffocated by her parents' protectiveness, she used the money to start her travels around the world.

Now here she is, two years later, in Rio de Janeiro, looking down the barrel of a gun.

'You're going to kill us, aren't you?' Katrina says.

The man lowers the gun. 'No, I'm not going to kill you. The American, is he here?'

'No, he left. You . . . ' Katrina's voice catches. Now that he has lowered the gun, and it seems like they might not die after all, ironically the fear comes back. 'You're Kubaschi, aren't you?'

'No, I'm not Kubaschi. Kubaschi's dead. I should know; I helped bury him.'

Jay takes a step forward. 'Now hold on just a minute — '

The man lifts his arm and points the

gun at Jay. 'Stay there, mister. I know who the girl is — Katrina Maslow — but about you I know very little, apart from the fact that you run the adventure business down on the harbour. What's your name?'

'Jay Stone.'

'Yeah? You know I got that much off the sign over your door. J's your initial. What's your full name?'

Jay shrugs, looking embarrassed. 'You really don't wanna know.'

'What's all this about?' Katrina says.

'I can't tell you that right now.' The man lowers the gun, apparently deciding that Jay doesn't pose a threat after all. 'You two are going to have to come with me.'

'What, just like that, because you say so?' Jay says. 'We don't even know who you are.'

'It doesn't matter who I am. I have a car outside, and we need to leave now. You are both in danger here. I will be taking you somewhere safe, to meet someone.'

'Who?' Katrina says.

'You'll see.'

Katrina looks at Jay. She can see the suspicion she feels, reflected in his eyes. But really, what choice do they have?

She takes a deep breath. 'Okay, we'll come with you.'

* * *

Stahl, standing in the shadows of a narrow alleyway, watches them leave. Katrina has her handbag with her, the strap slung over her shoulder. The man takes them to his truck, a four-door Ford F150.

*Typical US government issue*, Stahl thinks, watching the man drive off, weaving slowly through the crowds of late-night revellers. *Does this town ever stop partying?*

His plan had been to go and get his gun from his briefcase, hidden in a false bottom in the boot of the Corvette. Once back in Katrina's apartment he had planned to shoot the boyfriend, and then retrieve the USB stick. Stahl knows he has acted foolishly, letting his desires get ahead of his mission. All that fooling around, taking her out to dinner, telling her scare stories about Kubaschi, the dead hitman. Those stories had served their purpose with Lowenstein — until the old man rumbled him, that is — but Stahl had just been trying to scare Katrina, have some fun with her. That's the way it should have gone down. But the bitch had to go and spoil it all by fighting back.

Now he knows better.

He should have found the USB stick first, and then had his fun with Katrina later.

Stahl gingerly touches the scratches on his face with his fingertips. They come away bloody.

Stepping out of his hiding place, he moves through the crowd, heading for his car. He knows this is his last chance now. If the information on that USB stick falls into the wrong hands, there will be hell to pay.

Stahl doesn't intend to make the same mistake again. This time he will make sure he has what he needs, and then he will have his way with that stupid girl.

After what she has done to him, he deserves whatever he can take.

* * *

As they drive through town, Jay absent-mindedly rubs his sore stomach. He looks out of his tinted window at the couples walking past them, holding hands, or with arms around each others' shoulders. They look happy, relaxed, carefree. Most of them will be tourists, out enjoying the Rio nightlife. They have no idea what's going on in their midst, and Jay feels envious of them. What a strange night this is turning out to be. All Jay wanted to do was come back to Katrina's apartment and talk with her. He wanted to tell her how he feels about her, about how that woman she saw him with means nothing to him.

But he never had the chance. And now that is paling into insignificance, compared to the mess they have found themselves in. Jay glances over at Katrina, her head turned away from him as she looks out of her window.

There a few people extremely interested in her, but why? It seems to Jay that all of this started when Katrina met the old man on the bus the day she was late for work. When was that? Yesterday? No, the day before. Then, when the old man died on her in Baronetti's, everything just seemed to have gone strange, in a big way. But why? What's the connection? Does Stahl think that Katrina has something of his, or something he wants that the old man had and passed on to Katrina?

But Katrina certainly doesn't seem to think that she possesses anything of the scientist's, or that he ever handed anything over to her. And now this guy — driving them to a meeting with someone who, Jay gets the feeling, they might actually recognise.

One thing Jay knows for sure. He's going to do his damndest to protect her. Finding her in the apartment like that, fighting off Stahl, made him realise how much she means to him.

Jay won't let anybody else hurt her.

# 19

They start heading upwards. Katrina recognises the road they are on: it leads up Corcovado Mountain, finishing at the statue of Christ the Redeemer. In daylight hours the mountain is full of tourists. They travel up in cars, or on trams, or they hike through the rain-forest, all to see the statue, listed as one of the seven wonders of the world.

Now the road is eerily deserted, the truck's headlamps the only illumination as they drive through the Tijuca forest.

In the months she has been resident in Rio, Katrina has never visited the statue — one of those things she has always intended to do, but never got around to. She wishes she was heading there in happier circumstances now.

*What have I got myself involved in?* she wonders, as the car slips quietly through the forest. She thinks of her first meeting with Oliver Lowenstein on the bus, racking her brain for anything he might have said to her. First Ben Stahl, and now this man; both seem to think she has something important, something worth chasing her for, and fighting over. But what?

Did Lowenstein pass something on to her, like an athlete passing on the baton in a race? She only saw him twice — the first time on the bus, and then when he fell into her arms in the Baronetti. Neither time did he ask her to help him in any way, or look after something for him.

But then why did he mention her name as he was dying? Not once, but three times, if Detective Benzali was to be believed.

The thought of the detective's corpse lying under her bed while she slept on the mattress, separated from him by only a few feet, sends a shiver through her. She feels sad, too. Katrina liked the kindly detective, and the thought of him dying at the hands of Stahl upsets her.

Jay takes her hand in his and gives it a gentle squeeze. Katrina squeezes his hand in return, the only form of communication they need in the darkness of the car. She feels reassured by his presence, and can think of no one else she would rather have with her right now, facing whoever it is they are being taken to meet at the top of the mountain.

Soon they are turning a corner and the Ford's headlights illuminate the base of the massive statue. Parked in the car park is another car, a huge sedan, its headlights on full beam, silhouetting the man standing in front of it.

Katrina is suddenly certain that they are going to die, that this has all been a ruse to get them out of the city and somewhere remote, where they can be disposed of without any fuss or witnesses. They were stupid to come along so willingly, to be led somewhere they cannot raise the alarm. Tomorrow morning the first of the tourists will ascend the mountain to see the famous statue of Christ, and they will find two dead bodies lying at the foot of the redeemer.

They pull up in front of the other car, the two sets of headlights casting a pool of bright light in between their bumpers.

'Time to get out,' the man says.

They all climb out of the truck, Katrina and Jay holding their hands up to shield their eyes from the harsh light. The man they saw standing silhouetted in front of his car steps forward, so that his face is illuminated. It takes Katrina a few long moments before she realises where she has seen him before.

'You're the politician,' she says. 'I saw you on TV.'

He holds a hand out in greeting. 'Everett McCluskey, Under Secretary of State for the Environment. Please forgive me for the, shall we say, rather unique circumstances in which we meet. All very cloak-and-dagger, I know — feels like we are in the middle of a

Hollywood B-movie — but we have important matters to talk over and,' he glances up at the statue of Christ, 'this seemed the most appropriate place, as we could surely do with a little divine intervention right now.' He turns his attention to Jay and raises an eyebrow. 'Now, I know all about Katrina Maslow, but you, sir — I know nothing about you, or why you're here.'

Even in these suspicious, threatening circumstances, Katrina has to suppress a smile as she sees Jay pull himself up a little straighter and puff out his chest, as though trying to make himself appear an individual not to be messed with.

'J Stone, and don't even ask what the J stands for, as I ain't telling you.'

'You don't have to tell us, young man. A simple search on one of our databases will tell us everything we need to know about you. The only thing that matters to me right now is, are you our friend, or enemy?'

Jay takes hold of Katrina's hand

again. 'Depends. If you're intending to hurt Katrina, then I am most definitely your enemy.'

'You've got guts, son, I'll give you that. But you're stupid, too. Never mind, we're all friends here.' McCluskey pauses for a moment, seeming to size them up. 'Has Tom given you any indication as to why you are here?'

'If you mean the man who drove us up here, no.'

A mobile phone starts bleeping, and the man called Tom pulls a phone out of his pocket and answers it in a low voice. He walks away into the darkness, talking quietly.

'Katrina,' McCluskey says, pulling her attention back to him. 'Do you have any idea at all why you are here? I want you to think now. Anything you can remember may be of the utmost importance.'

'Does all of this have anything to do with Oliver Lowenstein?'

'Indeed it does.' McCluskey pauses again, as if unsure how to proceed. 'Did you know Professor Lowenstein at all?'

'No, I only met him a couple of days ago. We were on the same bus; it was stuck behind the protesters. Being the only English people on the bus, we started talking.'

'And did he give you anything whilst you were talking? Did he ask you to look after something for him?'

Katrina sighs. There is a gentle breeze, and it is cool on her face. She is aware of the statue of Jesus towering over them, watching over the city. As a child she attended Sunday school every week and used to believe that Jesus watched over her every move, protecting her from harm. Standing beneath the statue of the redeemer now, she offers up a silent prayer for help — that they might survive this night, and extricate themselves from this nightmare.

'No,' she says, finally. 'He never asked me to do him any sort of favour at all.'

'What's all this about?' Jay says. 'Why are you so interested in the old man?'

'Professor Lowenstein was a fugitive,' McCluskey replies. 'He was on the run, not only from his former employers, but from several different law enforcement agencies.'

'I don't understand,' Katrina says. 'He seemed like such a nice old man. I can't imagine him committing a crime.'

McCluskey gives her a sad smile. 'You're right, young lady. Professor Lowenstein was an honourable, decent man. I had the privilege of meeting him several years ago when he was younger, fitter, and his wife was still alive. Happier times. We've been good friends ever since. Lowenstein was passionate about his life's work, and he devoted the later years of his life, when he should have been enjoying his retirement and reflecting on past glories, to continuing to follow that passion. His crime, if you can call it that, was one committed for noble reasons.' McCluskey points behind them. 'Look out there, and just pause a moment. Take in the view.'

Katrina and Jay both turn and observe the city below them, its lights twinkling and glowing in the darkness. Beyond the city is the dark, shimmering mass of the ocean, and beyond that is the purple of the night sky, punctured by the dazzling array of stars.

'It's beautiful, isn't it?' McCluskey says. 'Beautiful and fragile. I'm here for the climate conference, representing one of the most powerful countries in the world. The United States has a responsibility to stand up and take action to help protect our beautiful, fragile planet. Hell, we all have a responsibility to do that, every single one of us, but the USA needs to be seen to be standing up and playing its part more than anybody else.

'That's why I'm here at the conference. Did you know, this forest you drove through to get here was hand-planted in the nineteenth century? The tourists come here and they think it's an ancient rainforest, one of the last surviving examples of its kind in Brazil.

But it's not ancient at all; it's less than 200 years old. The original rainforest that grew here had been destroyed to make way for coffee farms. In the second half of the nineteenth century, in an effort to protect the city from continual flooding, Major Manuel Gomez Archer instigated a scheme to replant the forest. Tijuca forest is now home to an incredible array of mammals and birds and plants, many threatened by extinction, and is designated a national park. Although he probably never realised it, Major Archer was ahead of his time, an early environmentalist. If he could return today and see what a mess we are making of our planet, he would be appalled, I'm sure.'

McCluskey pauses a moment, regarding Katrina and Jay thoughtfully. Katrina can hear Tom, still talking softly into his mobile.

'You're probably wondering what this history lesson has to do with you, aren't you?' McCluskey continues. 'Well, here's the thing. Professor Lowenstein and Major

Archer had much in common, the most important thing being this: they both saw a problem, and they both came up with a solution to that problem.'

Katrina shifts her feet. She is intrigued by where McCluskey is headed with this, but she is growing stiff and tired.

'Lowenstein had been employed by Coeus Petroleum as the environmentally friendly face of the company. You've probably never heard of Coeus — one of those invisible corporations behind the other big oil companies — but Coeus is a major player in the oil refinery business, and at times a major polluter too. Lowenstein was no fool; he knew exactly why he had been offered the job. He was there to make a company embattled by a series of environment-related public relations disasters look better, nothing more. But he took the job anyway. He felt he had a much better chance of influencing the oil industry into a more sustainable way of business from the inside, rather than as a thorn in their side.'

'But he did something to make them angry, didn't he?' Katina says. 'He did something they didn't like.'

'Well, not at first. To begin with they got along great. It was an unlikely meeting of minds, but Professor Lowenstein and the oil industry suddenly seemed as though they were a better fit than anybody could have imagined. Only three weeks before he went on the run, Lowenstein spoke at a press conference, in which Coeus committed itself to some important pledges to clean up its record on pollution. But then he discovered something which changed his whole perspective.'

'What do you mean?'

'Lowenstein's passion — his obsession, really, for the last twenty years — had been to discover a carbon-neutral power source, a way in which we could provide the world with all the energy it needs without the associated pollution and driving upwards of $CO_2$ levels. And he found one — or rather, he invented one. Just like Major Archer before him, he saw an environmental problem that had potentially catastrophic consequences, and he found a solution.'

Katrina turns as she hears Tom walking closer. He has finished talking on his mobile, and his face is grave. 'My people were closing in on Stahl; it appears he was trying to follow us. Unfortunately, they lost him.'

'But did you lose him, Tom?'

'No one followed us, sir. I made sure of that.'

'Then we have a little more time.' McCluskey looks at Katrina and Jay, again appearing to size them up, as if judging their moral character. 'Lowenstein had been working on this project whilst at Coeus. He had used their massive computing power — their funds, and in some cases their manpower. He presented his case to them — a unique opportunity for a globally powerful company to invest in green technology. Unfortunately, they didn't see it that way. What the management board of Coeus saw was the loss of billions of dollars already invested in oil. Lowenstein's technology had such far-reaching potential for change in the way in which we source our energy, that it scared them. They immediately ordered all of Lowenstein's files to be obliterated, his computer hard drives to be wiped, his prototypes to be destroyed.'

'But that's wrong,' Katrina says. 'Why did they do that?'

'Profit margins, Katrina. For them it always comes down to profit margins. People like them aren't interested in the pursuit of knowledge, of thinking forward beyond their own lives, or their own circle. They are simply chasing the mighty dollar. Lowenstein became a hounded man. He was forced out of his job, his home was burgled, and even his former colleagues were threatened — warned against associating with him. Of course, none of this was attributable to Coeus. As far as they were concerned, Lowenstein and Coeus had come to an amicable parting of the ways.'

'How do you know all this?'

'Lowenstein contacted me just last

week. Told me everything. Said he was scared, that he was being followed, that he feared for his safety. I asked him why. If Coeus had effectively destroyed his design, his invention, it would take him years to redesign it, so their investment was safe for the time being. But Lowenstein still had a copy of his files — his research, the design template, everything he needed to make it public. He had it all stored on a USB stick, and he was bringing it to Rio, to present at the conference and make it public. I agreed to meet him here, asked Tom to collect him. Unfortunately, the stress of the last few months had obviously been too much for Professor Lowenstein, and his paranoia levels had ratcheted up to extreme levels. Anytime Tom got near him, the professor fled, believing, I suppose, that Tom was an agent of the enemy. He went to ground, and we lost him.'

Tom, who has been standing next to Katrina, looking out over the city lights, suddenly grunts and sits down on the bonnet of McCluskey's car. At first, Katrina cannot understand what she is seeing, as a rough circle of red blossoms and spreads over Tom's chest. Then, as McCluskey grabs Katrina and Jay and hauls them both to the ground, she realises that he has been shot.

'Get down!' the politician hisses.

Tom slides to the floor and grunts again. He pulls his gun out, his face contorted in a grimace at the pain. 'Crawl under the truck; we're lit up like a Christmas tree in these headlights.'

Katrina can't help but stare at Tom, frozen at the sight of the blood staining his shirt. There's just so much of it.

'Move!' Tom hisses.

Katrina jumps as Jay grabs her hand and pulls her towards the truck. They squeeze underneath it, her back scraping against the underside of the Ford, the stink of oil filling her nostrils. McCluskey crawls in behind them.

'What about Tom?' Katrina says.

McCluskey drags himself up beside Katrina, his face tight and old-looking in the shadows cast by the other car's headlight beams. 'Tom is a US agent. He can look after himself.'

They all flinch as the Ford's windscreen shatters. Katrina knows it can only be Stahl out there. Somehow he found them, followed them without Tom realising. He's hiding in the darkness of the forest with a rifle, intent on picking them off. Katrina crawls further under the truck as another window shatters above them, the glass showering on the ground beside her.

'He's got us pinned down,' Jay says. 'We'll never get out of here alive if we just lie here.'

McCluskey pulls a mobile out of a hidden pocket, his movements awkward in the confined space under the Ford. The screen lights up as he punches in a series of numbers, and he holds his hand around the phone to screen the glow. 'We need backup, now! We've got a man down, and we are under fire. Get your people up here now, dammit!'

Katrina can see Tom slowly pulling

himself around the car, dragging himself out of the pool of light cast by the headlamps. His breathing is laboured, but he is still clutching his gun. He looks back at the others before he disappears into the darkness. 'Stay there until I start shooting. Then get in the truck, and get out of here as fast as you can.'

'What about you?' Katrina says.

'Don't worry about me.' Tom pauses, coughs, and spits. His breathing sounds even more laboured than before. 'Once you drive off, Stahl will lose interest in me, and he'll be straight after you.'

'Help's on the way, Tom,' McCluskey hisses. 'Just hang in there, okay?'

Tom nods and crawls out of the pool of light, his booted feet the last they see of him as he drags himself into the darkness.

They wait in silence, the minutes dragging out like hours. Stahl has stopped shooting at them, and Katrina wonders if he has a plan — if he is circling around them, ready to start firing at them from a different angle. The silence is more oppressive, more frightening, than the shooting had been. Katrina's heart is thumping so hard in her chest that she fears everyone can hear it; that Stahl could locate them in the darkness from the sound of that alone.

Suddenly the shooting starts up again, but this time it's Tom, his handgun blazing away in the darkness. Stahl starts firing back, and McCluskey grunts and says, 'That's our cue. Let's get going.'

The last thing Katrina wants to do right now is crawl out from under the relative safety of her hiding place and back into the open. But McCluskey is already hauling himself across the tarmac surface; and Jay, perhaps sensing her reluctance, has grabbed her arm.

'Come on, quick!'

They slide out from under the truck. McCluskey, crouching low, reaches up and pulls open the driver's side door. Keeping down, he crawls into the cab, sliding over the seats so that he can't be seen through the shattered windscreen. Katrina and Jay are both fully out from under the Ford now, and she feels exposed.

Katrina freezes as silence drops over them again. Slowly, Jay reaches up and pulls at the rear door handle. The sound the door mechanism makes as it disengages reverberates through the quiet night, and Katrina is certain that Stahl must have heard it and realised what they are doing.

Jay swings the door open and Katrina crawls in first, keeping down between the front and back seats. Jay slides along the back seats, leaning back to shut the door behind him. Katrina screams as the rear window shatters, showering her in tiny shards of glass.

The Ford's engine roars into life, the vehicle shuddering as McCluskey struggles to shift into reverse.

'Come on, you tub of — '

Suddenly they are moving, McCluskey spinning the steering wheel, reversing them around in a tight circle. Katrina, lying on her front in the rear footwell, pushes herself onto her elbows and knees, and peers through the gap between the front seats. The trees of the Tijuca forest are lit up in the sweeping glow of the headlights as the truck turns. Another window shatters, and Katrina throws herself on the floor again. She can hear McCluskey swearing as he struggles with the gear stick, fighting to get it into first. The gears crunch, the engine almost stalls, and then the wheels are spinning, fighting for traction for what seems like an age, before the vehicle shoots forward.

Katrina hears and feels the engine roar as McCluskey shoves his foot down on the gas pedal. The Ford judders and kangaroos, and the gears crunch again as he fights to change up and get the truck under control. Katrina yelps as her head is whipped back and hits a metal strut. She can see Jay's shadowed form as he fights to stay on the seat and not get thrown off and land on top of her.

The truck jerks forward, and something lands on Katrina's face. She grabs at it as they begin careering down the mountain road. It is her handbag, and she clutches it tight, suddenly overcome with a feeling that it contains what they are looking for. The thing that everybody is after, the key to this whole mess.

The Ford lurches sideways and then levels out again as McCluskey pulls them back into the middle of the carriageway. *We're going to make it!* Katrina thinks as they hurtle downwards, away from Stahl and his rifle. There is the crack of another gunshot, and the truck lurches violently to the left. A sudden thudding and rumbling fills the night.

'He shot the rear tyre out!' McCluskey shouts. 'Hold on, I'm gonna keep driving!'

The rumbling stops only seconds after it started, to be replaced with a horrendous screeching as the last of the tyre disintegrates, and the metal wheel grinds against the tarmac road. From her lying position on the floor of the car, Katrina can see sparks flying, bright yellow and orange against the night sky. McCluskey doesn't even pause, pushing the truck's speed up as much as he can. Katrina claps her hands over her ears, feeling she can't take the horrible noise much longer.

# 20

McCluskey slams on the horn, the strident sound cutting through the noise of the clubbers, sending them scattering and screaming. Katrina and Jay are sitting up in the back seat, now that they are back down from the mountain, but Katrina keeps closing her eyes. McCluskey is not slowing down, even now, back in the centre of the city, and she is sure they are going to knock somebody over, maybe kill someone.

She screams at him to slow down, to stop, but the politician ignores her, swearing as people get in their way. McCluskey takes a tight corner, and they start rattling down a narrow alley, the walls on either side of them only inches from the car doors. People jump back into doorways, waving their fists and cursing at him as they surge past.

A line of washing, bed sheets hanging

so low their edges almost touch the ground, suddenly materializes in the light of the Ford's headlights. McCluskey swears as the bed sheets envelop the front of the truck, billowing in through the shattered windscreen and wrapping around the politician's head. He fights to free himself from the sheets, but too late. He loses control of the Ford and the left side grinds against the wall, slowing them to a stop.

'Out of the car!' McCluskey shouts, fighting to free himself from the bed sheets' embrace.

Jay opens his door, but it stops, hitting against the opposite wall, with only a five-inch-wide gap. 'There's no room! The alley is too narrow, we're trapped inside!'

'We can get out of the back,' Katrina says. The rear windscreen was shattered when Stahl fired at them earlier. Katrina wonders how close the bullet came to hitting any of them. She grabs her handbag, slipping the strap over her shoulder.

Jay gives her an odd look. 'This is no

time to be worrying about your handbag.'

Katrina slips the strap off her shoulder again. 'Actually, this is just the time to be worrying about my handbag.' She opens it up and dumps the contents on the seat.

'Katrina, what on earth are you doing? We need to get out of here!'

McCluskey wins his battle with the bed sheets, resurfacing at last, and twists around in his seat. 'Jay's right, we need to leave before Stahl catches up with us.'

'Just wait a second, will you?' With the bag now completely empty, Katrina scrunches the soft material up in her hands, feeling for something unfamiliar, something wrong with her handbag. She looks at Jay, and then at McCluskey. 'There! I found it.' She reaches inside her bag, pinches at the lining, and pulls until it starts to rip. The two men watch in silence as she reaches inside the torn lining and pulls out a silver USB stick.

'Dear God, you found it,' McCluskey whispers.

'Lowenstein did pass this onto me, after all.' Katrina is suddenly overcome with emotion, as she imagines the old man entrusting her, the only friendly person he knew right then, with this important information.

'But when?' Jay says.

Katrina takes a deep breath, regaining her composure. 'It must have been at the Baronetti, when he collapsed against me. The lining had been ripped in my handbag earlier in the day, when I had to push my way through the crowds of protesters. It got pretty hairy in there — there was a lot of shoving and pushing — and someone made a grab for my bag, and the lining got ripped as I yanked it off them. When Lowenstein dropped the USB stick in there, it must have fallen in between the lining and the outer material. The next day I sewed it up, never noticing the USB stick.'

McCluskey holds out his hand. 'Katrina, I think you need to give that to me.'

'He's found us,' Jay says.

The truck's cab is filling up with light, casting deep shadows across the seats and the dashboard. They all turn and look as a car, headlights on full beam, hurtles towards them, careening off the sides of the narrow alleyway.

'Oh no, he's going to ram us,' Katrina whispers.

For a moment they are all frozen as they watch the headlights growing larger and brighter, as Stahl hurtles closer. But then they spring into action. Katrina and Jay squirm over the front seats after McCluskey as he hauls himself through the shattered front window. Katrina drags herself onto the truck's bonnet, the sharp edges of the windscreen scratching her stomach. McCluskey rolls off the bonnet and onto the cobbled ground. Katrina is almost completely out, Jay just behind her, when the Corvette slams into the back of the Ford, throwing them violently off the bonnet.

As she slams into the cobble stones on her front, her chest feeling like it is caving in under the impact, the USB stick flies from her hand and goes spinning into the dark. Jay is beside her on his back, now rolling over and scrambling to his feet. Katrina can hear the high-pitched whine of the Corvette's engine.

Jay reaches down and grabs Katrina's arm, hauling her to her feet. 'He's backing up. He's going to ram us again!'

'I've lost the USB stick!'

Katrina looks around, desperately trying to find it amongst the shadows cast by the beam of light from the Ford's headlamps. She falls down onto her knees and starts patting the ground with her hands, as though she is searching for a contact lens. It can't have fallen far; she's sure it has to be somewhere close by. After everything that has happened, and the price Lowenstein paid for keeping it out of Stahl's hands, she hates the idea of losing it now.

'Katrina!' Jay hisses, crouching down beside her. 'Leave it. We've got to get moving.'

'I need to find that USB stick. We can't leave without it.'

'We don't have time!'

As if on cue, they hear the Corvette's engine note shift, and then grow louder as it speeds down the narrow alley toward them once more. On the edge of panic, Katrina widens her search, stretching out her arms and letting her palms glide over the rough surface of the street's cobblestones.

'The young man is right,' McCluskey says, reaching down and grabbing Katrina by the arm. 'Our lives are worth far more than a few microchips, regardless of the information they might contain.'

'Got it!' Katrina's fingers close around the metal tube, just as McCluskey yanks her upright. Together, the three of them lunge forward, running down the alley as the Corvette smashes into the truck's rear in an explosion of grinding metal, shoving it forward into the spot they just left.

McCluskey stops Katrina and Jay as they reach the end of the alley. 'Stahl will have the same problem as us — he can't open his doors. How long do you think he'll be trapped in his car?'

'No time at all.' Katrina says. 'He's got a fold-down roof; he can just climb out.'

'Okay.' McCluskey pulls a gun from a jacket pocket and glances down the alley. 'You two run on ahead. I'll see if I can take care of Stahl, or slow him down at least.'

Jay stares wide-eyed at the pistol in McCluskey's hand. 'What kind of a politician are you?'

The older man grins. 'The kind that likes to take a hands-on approach to the job. Now get out of here!'

They don't need telling again, but turn and run into the crowds on the main thoroughfare, losing themselves in the mass of humanity wandering through the centre of town. Katrina clutches the silver USB stick tight in her fist, knowing she will never give it up to Stahl.

# 21

Half an hour later and they are standing by the bar in a club, holding each other tight. Katrina is shivering, with shock she supposes, and she can feel Jay's body coiled with tension. Both of them are keeping an eye on the front entrance. After walking aimlessly through the city streets, they decided to hide in the darkness and crowds of a night club whilst they thought about what to do next. They both bought a drink, but they have not touched them.

Katrina puts her mouth close to Jay's ear, the deafening music making it difficult to be heard. 'We should go to the police.'

Jay shakes his head. 'I don't think that's a good idea. Stahl seems unstoppable, and we don't know how much firepower he's got.'

'The police can get us somewhere

safe. They can protect us.'

'I don't know. I know what you're saying, and it's the obvious thing to do, but I don't like it. Once we get the police involved, we'll be pinned down. I think our best bet right now is to get moving again and keep out of Stahl's reach.'

'But what else are we going to do? We can't spend the whole night running, hiding in clubs. Even in Rio, the clubs shut at some point.'

Jay's brow creases — with worry, or because he is concentrating, Katrina cannot tell. 'We need to get somewhere safe, somewhere he'll never find us.'

A girl screams and Katrina flinches, looking wildly around. She can see a young woman laughing, and she screams again as her boyfriend lifts her into the air.

Jay nuzzles his head against Katrina's. She can feel his warm breath on her cheek and her ear. 'I know where we can go.'

Katrina looks at him and raises her

eyebrows. Jay just smiles and takes her hand, and they push their way through the men and women dancing and drinking, and back outside.

They walk for another hour, Jay taking them on a circuitous route back to Katrina's apartment. They both glance behind themselves constantly, convinced Stahl is going to leap out at them at any moment. Katrina is not convinced that they should go back to her apartment; she is scared that the American will be waiting for them when they get there. But Jay manages to convince her it will be okay. He doesn't want to go inside her apartment, or even in the building.

'I parked my truck around the corner when I came to see you earlier. We just need the truck, and then we're going for a drive.'

'But where to?'

'You'll see.'

By the time they find the truck, the streets are emptying, as even the most die-hard partygoers start thinking about returning home and going to bed. Katrina climbs wearily into the cab beside Jay, lets her head fall back against the seat head-rest, and closes her eyes.

The engine roars into life and Jay squeezes her hand. 'Not long now, and we'll be safe.'

Katrina opens her eyes and twists her head, still leaning against the head-rest, and looks at Jay. 'Thank you for everything.'

'Don't mention it. I've had a ball.'

'You're an idiot,' Katrina says, and smiles.

Jay laughs and shifts the gearstick into first. He slowly eases the truck out onto the main road. Neither of them notices the shadowy figure quickly climbing onto the bed of the truck, and lying down amongst the scuba-diving and caving gear.

# 22

'You cannot be serious.'

'Why not? This is the best idea I've ever had.'

The ticking of the cooling engine is the only noise they hear as they sit in the cab, looking out of the truck's now stationary windscreen.

'I can't do this.' Katrina shifts uncomfortably in her seat, but she cannot take her eyes off the sight before them.

'Yes you can.'

'No, I can't.'

'Come on, Katrina, of course you can do this. You're fearless.'

Katrina sighs. How was he to know? Of course he couldn't, because she never told him.

The DHC-6 Twin Otter sits on the airfield before them, on the other side of the chain-link fence, seeming almost to mock Katrina with its beauty and power. Katrina knows all about the Twin Otter: that they are Canadian built aircraft, they can carry nineteen passengers, they are famous for their short takeoff and landing abilities — known in the profession as STOL — and that they are used around the world by commercial skydiving schools.

But for Katrina, the sight of the Twin Otter will always remind her of the last time she saw her beloved Pete, as he leapt into the void at 12,000 feet.

'Katrina? What's wrong? Are you crying?'

Katrina wipes a hand roughly across her eyes, feeling cross with herself. How much longer does she have to carry this burden around with her? How many more years does she have to mourn for her lost fiancé? Of course she loved him, and will always love him, but doesn't she have a right to live her own life now? Wouldn't Pete want her to move on and leave the past behind?

Katrina takes a deep, ragged breath,

and gives Jay a weak smile. 'I'm sorry. You must think I'm pathetic. No, worse — you probably think I'm a nutcase.'

'Never,' Jay says, taking her hand and giving it a reassuring squeeze. He looks into her eyes and Katrina feels like she is high above the earth once more, ready to fall, to endlessly plummet through the atmosphere. Her stomach turns over with the giddy sensation of vertigo even though she is sitting in a truck, on solid ground.

'Katrina,' Jay says. 'Katrina, I . . . '

'Yes, I know.' Katrina runs her fingertips softly down his cheek. In her mind's eye she is back in the air again, with Pete. But this time it is Katrina who leaps out of the aeroplane first, leaving Pete behind, and she falls, twisting and turning; and it is glorious and wonderful, and she is free. 'I love you too.'

'You do?' Jay says, and he smiles like a kid on Christmas morning, spying the pile of presents under the Christmas tree.

'Aww, now ain't this sweet?' Stahl is standing outside the cab, a gun trained on them. Katrina stares at him, her mind unable to comprehend what she is seeing. How did he find them so quickly?

'Well, what are you waiting for?' He waves the gun at them. 'Get out.'

Katrina feels Jay tense up, and Stahl must see something in his stance too.

'Don't go trying anything funny, surfer dude. I ain't in the mood for dancing with you tonight. If you wanna have fun and games, I'll just shoot you in the head and get it over with.'

They climb out of the truck's cab, Stahl backing up to give them plenty of room, the gun never wavering, always pointing at Jay. Katrina still has the USB stick clutched tight in her fist. She realises she has not let it go since finding it on the cobblestones in the alley, and her hand starts to feel as though it might cramp up.

Stahl waves the gun at them, indicating they should walk around to the front of the truck. 'Put your hands on the hood.'

They both put their hands on the warm metal, Katrina's left hand still closed around the USB stick. Stahl notices it.

'Open your hand.'

Katrina cannot move; she cannot obey Stahl's instruction. She thinks of Professor Lowenstein, falling into her arms in the Baronetti; dying in a night-club in a foreign city, when he should have been at home in England, enjoying his retirement. She thinks of the risks he took, the price he paid, to keep the knowledge of his world-changing invention alive and out of the wrong hands. How can she give it up so easily? How can it end like this?

Stahl takes a step forward, pointing the gun at her head. 'Open your hand.'

Slowly, painfully, Katrina turns her hand over and uncurls her fingers. Her finger joints feel like rusty hinges, creaking and grinding after years spent closed. Her hand opens fully, and lying in her palm is the USB stick.

'Put it on the hood,' Stahl says.

Katrina carefully places the metal tube on the truck's bonnet. She feels as though she is committing a dreadful crime, betraying a man she hardly knew, and yet still the betrayal cuts deep.

'Back up, away from the truck.'

Katrina and Jay step back, and as they do, Jay slips his hand into Katrina's. Again, despite the fear, she experiences a giddy sensation of vertigo. She is weightless, suddenly free of a terrible burden she has been carrying around with her for years.

Why has she found out now that she is still capable of love, when it might be too late? All this time she has been living with her memories of her fiancé, and letting those memories stop her from experiencing life afresh. This is not what he would have wanted, she is sure now. Pete would want to her to move on, to live her life; Katrina is overwhelmingly convinced of that.

She just hopes she hasn't come to that realisation too late.

Stahl takes the USB stick off the truck's bonnet and slips it into his pocket. 'Good, good,' he mutters, looking thoughtful, still pointing the gun at Katrina. 'Now, let's think about this. Let's consider our options. What we ideally need here is a win-win situation, right?'

'You'll never get away with this,' Jay says.

'You know, it's funny,' Stahl says, breaking into a big, cheesy grin, 'but Detective Benzali said exactly the same thing to me earlier today, just before I shot him between the eyes.'

'I hate you!' Katrina spits the words out, not wanting to antagonise him, but unable to control herself.

Stahl giggles. 'That's a real crying shame. You and me, we could have made sweet music together. A little bit of the old bump and grind, some . . . '

'Shut up!' Jay snaps. 'You leave her alone.'

Stahl swings the gun around, until it

is pointing at Jay's head. 'Quiet, lover-boy. When I want to hear you talk, I'll ask you a question. All right? Until then, you keep shtum.'

Stahl looks from one to the other of them and his smile, if possible, gets bigger. Behind the American, Katrina can see the stars and a full moon shining brightly against the purple of the night sky. On the horizon she can just make out the first pink tinges promising the dawn to come. And with the promise of that new day, she feels a flicker of hope ignite in her chest. *We might get out of this alive, yet.*

'Now listen up, kids. I've got a plan — one that will work for your benefit just as much as mine.'

'Yeah? What's that?' Jay says. Katrina can hear the tension and the hate in his voice. She wills him to keep his anger under control. They need to keep Stahl happy and calm. It's the only chance they have of getting out of this alive.

'You're going to fly me out of here.'

Jay laughs — a single, explosive bark

of laughter. 'You're crazier than you look. What makes you think I'm going to help you escape?'

'Because it's the only way your pretty little girlfriend lives to see tomorrow, that's why, blondie.'

'You think I can just fly you anywhere you want? There are aviation laws and restrictions on airspace we can fly through; restrictions on where we can land. We can't just pick you up and fly you wherever you want.'

'Don't give me any of that. I heard you plotting to escape just now. I know you can fly this bird out of here. Now let's get moving before I get tired of holding this gun. My trigger finger's getting mighty twitchy, if you get my meaning.'

'And you promise you'll let us go when we land?' Katrina says.

'Of course I will. I've got what I need; all I want now is a way out of here. Once I've got that, you're no more use to me.' Stahl leers at Katrina. 'Unless, of course, you decide I'm too irresistible to let go, and you can't help but ditch this loser and run away with me. I can show you a real good time, baby.'

'I'll pass,' Katrina says, unable to keep the revulsion out of her voice.

'Yeah, well, your loss. Let's get moving.'

# 23

Jay has a key for the padlock on the gate to the airfield. He doesn't have any more keys, but the simple lock on the Twin Otter's door presents no problem to him, and neither does the ignition.

If you know what you are doing, and can fly, then stealing a plane is easier than stealing a car, it seems to Katrina. Stahl keeps his gun trained on them the whole time.

The Twin Otter makes short work of climbing into the sky, and sitting next to Jay in the cockpit, Katrina can see a sliver of the orange sun breaking over the horizon. She had feared that even the simple act of climbing into the aircraft — the feel of it, its familiarity, the smell of the oil and the diesel — would reduce her to a quivering wreck. She was scared that she would have flashbacks of Pete's terrifying plunge to earth, the last time she saw him alive.

But she is calm and at peace. In the air once more, Rio de Janeiro below them, she is surprised at how much she has missed the sensation of flying. She is aware of Stahl standing behind them, the gun still in his hand, still pointing at them. How awful to have an agent of death lurking behind her, when she has never felt so alive. Whatever happens next, she knows she will find comfort in facing it with Jay next to her.

'Get me to Sao Paulo,' Stahl growls. 'And no funny stuff. I'm watching you all the time.'

'You'll never get past airport security when we land,' Jay says.

'Then find us somewhere to land where they won't ask any questions, flyboy.'

Jay shakes his head, and again Katrina wills him to keep calm, to hold his peace. They just need to keep Stahl happy. She wonders if it is possible to distract him.

'Just one thing I want to know. What did you do with Everett McCluskey?'

'The politician? I gave him the slip. I did consider shooting him just for the fun of it, but that would have hit the news in a big way. Too big. My orders are to do this as quietly as possible, luckily for him.'

'And you don't consider murdering a police detective will make the news?' Jay says.

Stahl shrugs. 'It's Rio. Happens all the time.'

Jay makes a few adjustments to his flight path, and glances back at Stahl. 'How can you live with yourself?'

'Easy. The money I earn on these jobs helps me live with myself very well. I've got the kind of lifestyle you can only dream about, flyboy.'

'But no friends, no family, no meaning to your life?'

'None of that matters to me.'

'But the things you've done, the people you've hurt and killed. Doesn't that weigh on your conscience? How do you sleep at night?'

'I sleep just fine. People die all the time, blondie. Old people, young people, babies — everybody dies one day. What difference does it make when, or where, or how? Maybe I'm part of some cosmic plan, one of many agents of death carrying out instructions from a celestial lawgiver. Maybe Benzali was meant to die when he did; and if it hadn't been me who killed him, then maybe he would've got run over by a bus, or had a heart attack, or an aneurysm.'

'You're utterly deluded, Stahl. You'll get caught one day, and then you'll pay.'

'Yeah, yeah, yeah. Change the record, sonny Jim. You're starting to repeat yourself.' Stahl looks at Katrina. She tries to ignore him, staring ahead at the horizon, the lights of Rio twinkling in the grey half-light of the early morning.

'What about you, Katrina? You know the meaning of death more than most. You know what I'm talking about, don't you?'

'What do you mean?' Jay looks at

Katrina. His face looks lined with worry in the early morning light. 'Katrina?'

Katrina looks away from him, unable to speak. She was going to tell him; she wanted to tell him herself. This is the last thing she wanted — for Jay to find out about Pete like this.

'She hasn't told you, has she?' Stahl chuckles. 'Now, is this the right way to be starting a relationship? Couples really shouldn't have secrets from each other, now, should they? Well, not to begin with, anyway. Katrina? Would you like to tell him, or shall I?'

Katrina grinds her teeth together, trying to keep a lid on the rage and hatred she feels for Stahl right at this moment. She wants to kill him. She wants to snatch the gun from his hand and turn it on him, and see him beg for his life.

'Looks like it's up to me. You're not her first flyboy boyfriend, blondie. Katrina 'twenty seconds to freefall' Maslow was engaged to be married to a skydiving instructor, but unfortunately on their last jump together his parachute failed to open and, well, you can imagine the rest.' Stahl is leaning forward now, between the two pilot seats. He points down and whistles, finishing off with, 'Splat!'

'You bastard!' Katrina screams, and lunges for his gun.

The gun discharges, punching a hole in the windscreen. The aircraft lurches to one side, and they are all thrown off balance. Katrina has both hands wrapped around Stahl's wrist, trying to lever his arm back and point the gun away. Jay glances at them wild-eyed, whilst trying to wrestle the Twin Otter onto a level flight path.

Stahl throws a punch at Katrina as the aeroplane lurches again, but his aim is off, and his fist connects with her sternum. She falls back, letting go of Stahl's arm, and hits her head on the control panel. Stahl is snarling, bringing the gun down to aim at her, when she kicks him in the stomach. He staggers, his lower legs hitting a seat, and he flips backwards, landing in a tangle between the seats.

'I'm turning round,' Jay says. 'Heading back to Rio. Try and get that gun off him!' He banks the aircraft steeply as they begin a tight turn.

Katrina hauls herself out of the cockpit. Stahl is lying in an awkward position, jammed in a gap between seats. For one triumphant moment she thinks he might have broken his arm, but then she realises he hasn't, as he starts to drag himself upright. His face is twisted with hate and utter rage, but he does not have the gun. Katrina glances around and sees it lying on the floor by the door. She lunges for it, but Stahl grabs her by the ankle and yanks hard. She smacks onto the cabin floor, her nose smashing into the hard surface. Her vision greys out for a moment, pain flooding through her skull.

Stahl climbs on her back and sits down, pinning her to the floor. He grabs her hands and twists them behind her back until she cries out with the pain. Locking her two wrists together with one hand, Stahl reaches out for the gun, lying just in front of Katrina's face. She tries to free herself, squirming under his weight, but he just forces himself down even more. The pain in her lower back, where he is sitting on her, is excruciating.

Stahl's fingertips are a fraction of an inch away from the gun when Katrina hears Jay shout, 'Get off her!' and the American collapses to the floor, letting go of her wrists. Katrina scrambles up, Jay helping her. Stahl looks up at them, blood trickling from his scalp, where Jay kicked him. The American twists and lunges for the gun, and Jay leaps on top of him. The two men fight on the floor, punching and kicking. Stahl grabs the Australian's long hair and pulls, and Jay wraps his hands around Stahl's neck, trying to strangle him. For one single, ridiculous moment, Katrina feels an urge to laugh hysterically, they look so funny.

Instead, she clambers over the seats and grabs the handgun off the floor. She points it at the two men.

'Stop.'

Neither of them hears her. Stahl has Jay's right arm pinned beneath his body, and is holding his left forearm. He looks as though he is trying to bite it.

'I said, *stop*!'

The two men stop fighting and look up.

Katrina sighs. 'That's better. Jay, I think you need to go back to flying the plane. I'll look after Stahl.'

Jay climbs unsteadily to his feet and looks at the gun in Katrina's hand. 'Are you okay with that thing?'

'I'm fine.' Katrina hopes her voice sounds steady enough. She doesn't feel fine, but she doesn't want Stahl to know that. 'How long until we get back to the airfield?'

'Only another minute or two.'

The pilotless aircraft suddenly lurches to one side and Katrina staggers, reaching out to steady herself. Before she has fully regained control, Stahl has slammed into her, smashing her into a locker door. Katrina collapses to the floor, the breath punched out of her body, the gun flying from her hand and skittering across the cabin.

The locker door springs open and packed parachutes tumble out and fall on top of Katrina, then thud to the floor. Stahl grabs the gun and swings it round to point at Jay, who was springing for him. Jay stops, lifting up his hands.

'Don't shoot. You still need me to get us back down on the ground.'

'Nah, I've got a better idea. Both of you step back, out of my way.'

Katrina and Jay back up, never taking their eyes off the American and his gun. Keeping the handgun levelled on them all the time, Stahl bends down and picks up a parachute. He slips his arms through the straps and starts fastening the buckles one-handed.

'I've never been skydiving before. Looks like it might be fun.'

'Don't be a fool, Stahl,' Jay says. 'You'll kill yourself.'

'How difficult can it be?' Stahl holds up the ripcord, his fingers curling around the plastic handle. 'I just jump out of the airplane and then pull this, right?' He grins. 'Oh, but I forgot one essential detail. First I shout 'twenty seconds to freefall', right?'

Stahl backs up to the door, keeping the gun levelled on Katrina and Jay all the time. He reaches out with his free hand and struggles with the door mechanism for a few moments. Finally he works it out, unlocks the door and swings it open.

Gusts of wind fill the cabin, whipping Katrina's hair into tangles around her face. She brushes it out of her eyes, expecting to see Stahl gone. But no, he is walking back into the cabin. One by one he picks up the other parachutes and throws them out of the door, until they are all gone.

'I was going to shoot you both, but I've got a better idea. I'm a nice guy, really. So I thought perhaps you might like to spend your final moments together, without me, to say your goodbyes.'

He swings the gun around and starts firing at the cockpit's control panel. Bits of plastic and glass erupt from the console, sparks flying and tiny flames flickering along the exposed wires. Stahl keeps firing until the gun clicks repeatedly, the clip empty, and then he throws the gun away.

The American grins, obviously enjoying himself. 'Well guys, it's been a blast, but I gotta go!'

Jay barrels into Stahl, throwing him to the floor. He scrambles on top of him and punches him in the face.

'You know what, Stahl? You talk too much!' He punches him again, and again. But then Stahl gets a leg up, gets some leverage under Jay, and knees him in the stomach. Suddenly they are both rolling to the open door.

'Jay!' Katrina screams.

Both men roll through the door, arms and legs tangled together. Jay manages to reach out for the metal doorframe, his fingers closing around it. For a heartbeat it seems as though he might be able to hang on, to halt his momentum.

But a moment later, both men are gone, and the doorway is empty.

Katrina is frozen in horror, staring at the empty space which Jay had filled a fraction of a second before. But for a moment what she sees is Pete falling gracefully through the air, his arms out as she falls above him. He is tugging at his ripcord, but the parachute is tangled; it won't open. She can see him tumbling, tumbling to the ground, until he disappears from view, and she knows he is dead.

The Twin Otter is listing to one side, losing power. The open doorway is down from, and in front of, her position by the locker. She can see the ground far below her. Katrina glances in the pilot's cabin. The control panel is ruined; not a chance the aircraft can be piloted to a safe landing. How long before it crashes depends on how well it can glide. Katrina has no idea.

And right now she doesn't care. All she can think of is Jay falling out of the aeroplane without a parachute. All she can see in her mind's eye are Jay and Stahl disappearing through the door.

How is it possible? Just when she has found love once more, after seeing her boyfriend plummet to his death, how can it happen again?

A picture of Christ the Redeemer, standing atop Corcovado Mountain, his arms outstretched in forgiveness and love, flashes into her mind.

*Please, help me*, she prays. *If you truly are a god of love and compassion, please give me strength and guidance when I need it the most. I cannot lose Jay, not when I have only just truly found him. I can't let it happen again!*

'I won't let it happen again!' she screams, and dives through the doorway into the void.

# 24

Katrina twists and turns, tumbling down, the wind pulling at her T-shirt and shorts, whipping her hair around her face. She is falling too fast, out of control. Her first instinct is to panic.

*What on earth was I thinking, leaping out of a plane without a parachute?*

But then she remembers why she did it. And she knows she can survive this, if she acts fast.

*Get your act together, girl! Come on, think!*

She straightens herself out, arching her back and throwing her arms out to the side, turning over onto her front. Her rate of descent slows down, and she is now falling steadily enough that she can look around.

There, below her, she can see Jay and Stahl, still in freefall. Jay has his arms wrapped around Stahl, clinging onto him like the lifeline he is. Stahl is throwing punches at Jay, trying to dislodge him as they twist and turn, their descent totally out of control. Behind them the city of Rio, lit up by the low dawn sun, provides a beautiful but frighteningly close backdrop.

Katrina tucks her chin into her chest, lays her arms flat along her sides, and goes into a dive. Her rate of descent increases dramatically, and she aims herself at the two figures below, imagining herself to be a bullet fired from a gun, shooting straight for them. Her long hair streams out behind her and her clothes ripple painfully against her skin, the sound like flags blowing in a gale.

Katrina tries calculating how long they have left to fall. She has no idea how high the aircraft was when they left it, but from up here it looks as though they were between 10,000 and 12,000 feet. If 10,000, then they have between forty and fifty seconds of freefall before they need to safely deploy a parachute.

The problem is, Stahl is the only one wearing a parachute.

Katrina draws closer to the two men, who are still tumbling and twisting out of control. Stahl is punching and kicking Jay, who is still hanging on, his arms wrapped around Stahl's waist. At the last moment, as she hurtles towards them, Katrina stretches out her arms, ready to grab onto anything she can as she smashes into them.

They collide with a sickening, bone-jolting thud. Jay almost lets go of Stahl, but Katrina grabs a handful of his shirt and pulls him closer. Her other hand finds a parachute strap, and she worms it in between the strap and Stahl's chest, securing herself to him as best she can.

The three of them spin erratically, and Katrina's vision is filled with ground, then sky, then ground again, over and over.

The cityscape of Rio looks frighteningly close now. Had they really been at 10,000 feet when they jumped? Maybe it was 8,000, maybe less.

'Let go of me!' Stahl screams, pushing and pulling at Katrina and Jay.

Katrina wraps her legs around the two of them, lets go of Jay and claws at Stahl's face, opening up the wounds she has already given him. With the heel of her hand she jabs at his nose, whipping his head back. She does it again, giving him no mercy.

'The buckles!' she yells at Jay. 'Undo the straps!'

Jay is still hanging on to Stahl. He can't do anything to help Katrina undo Stahl's harness without letting go of him.

How long left, before they have to deploy the 'chute? Thirty seconds, maybe?

Katrina's no longer sure; she is losing track of the time. All she knows is that the earth is hurtling towards them. Every time she sees the ground again, as she spins round and round, it seems a little closer, a little larger in her field of vision. Her left arm is entangled in part of Stahl's harness. With her right hand she was holding onto Jay, but she lets go, seeing that he is gripping hold of Stahl firmly.

Stahl starts struggling as he sees Katrina undoing one of his harness clips. He tries to grab her hair, but he is disoriented, and his arm flails at her, missing her head. The clip comes free, and she starts working on another one. Stahl punches her and, although there is not much power in it, it snaps her head sideways. If not for having slipped her arm inside Stahl's harness, wrapping it around her forearm, Katrina would have been knocked away, spinning downwards on her own.

Ignoring Stahl, Katrina undoes the clip. The lower part of his harness, round his pelvis and thighs, slips off him. Stahl screams, and Katrina can hear the panic in his voice.

How long left now? Twenty seconds? The ground comes into view again as they tumble round, and Katrina is shocked to see how close it looks. A lot less than twenty seconds left. Five, maybe seven or eight at the most.

Jay, seeing what Katrina is doing, has got a good, firm hold of part of Stahl's harness too, wrapping it around his arm so that, even if he lets go, he will still be caught up in it.

Katrina is reaching for the last safety clip when Stahl grabs her wrist and bends her arm back.

'If I'm gonna die, I'm taking you with me!' he snarls.

Jay, with his free hand, reaches up and snaps the clip open. Stahl slips from the harness, letting go of Katrina's wrist, but managing to hang on to a strap with one hand. He grabs her ankle and stares up at her, his lips curling back in an animal-like snarl. To Katrina, he no longer appears human.

'I'm going to kill you!' he screams.

She curls her free leg up, tucking her knee into her chest.

'Twenty seconds to freefall, you son of a — '

She kicks him in the face, snapping his head back. As he lets go of her ankle,

Katrina pulls the ripcord. The parachute opens, billowing out in a bright orange canopy, a shocking contrast against the dark blue of the sky. Their rate of descent slows down suddenly, from 130 to 13 miles per hour. Her arm feels as though it is being yanked from its socket, and Katrina and Jay are thrown around like puppets on strings.

Stahl, unable to hang on to the harness, is pulled earthwards by the force of gravity, continuing to fall at an incredible speed. Katrina looks away as he plummets toward the ground. As much as she hates him, she cannot watch him plunge to his death.

A gentle wind catches the parachute and pulls them along as they descend. They are both hanging from the parachute harness by one arm each, and have no control over where they are taken. They drift by the statue of Christ the Redeemer, narrowly missing one of his outstretched hands. He gazes benevolently upon them as they glide past his face.

*Lord, we just need a little more help, to get us safely on the ground. Just one more thing, okay?*

'Man, this is painful,' Jay croaks.

'I know,' Katrina replies.

Her shoulder feels like it is on fire. She pulls Jay close, and they wrap their free arms around each other as they float over the Tijuca forest, green and dense below them.

'Just a little longer,' she whispers.

Seconds later they are over Rio's infrastructure, the buildings and streets passing by below, and growing closer all the time. Katrina is growing anxious that their flight path will smash them into the side of a building, or they will get dragged along a busy main road and be run over by an early morning bus or delivery truck.

Katrina looks at Jay, his face only inches from hers. 'Whatever happens next, I just want you to know I love you, Jay.'

'I love you too, Katrina.'

Their lips meet, and they kiss.

And they continue kissing, ignoring the danger they are in, helpless to do anything about it. Katrina can hear people shouting as they see them floating down, and the traffic noise grows louder as they drop lower and lower.

Suddenly they are down, but the impact is nothing like Katrina expected. They are in water, being dragged through shallow surf, until they come to a halt. Katrina rolls over and looks shoreward, and bursts out laughing.

'Look where we landed!'

Jay starts laughing too. They are in Guanabara Bay, home of *J Stone Adventure Trips*.

Slowly, painfully, Katrina frees herself from the harness, and then helps Jay untangle himself too. She rolls him on his back in the water, and lies down on top of him.

And, as the surf gently breaks over them, she kisses him again.

# 25

Sunlight streams through the venetian blinds, enveloping Katrina's body in a warm glow. She tries rolling onto her back and groans as her body protests, her muscles crying out in agony, begging her to stay still. It seems as though every joint, every tendon and ligament, has something to say on the matter, too.

Opening her eyes and ignoring her body's commands to lie still, she pushes herself up into a sitting position. She is in a double bed in a spacious bedroom. Her clothes are lying in a pile beside the bed. She looks at the clock on the bedside cabinet.

2:56

In the afternoon, obviously, as the room is filled with sunlight.

But where is she?

Katrina leans back against the pillow,

too tired to even contemplate such an insurmountable task as climbing out of bed. Gazing idly around the bedroom, she allows the memories to start flooding back.

The fight with Stahl in her apartment, the drive up Corcovado Mountain to meet McCluskey, the flight in the Twin Otter, and the terrifying plunge through the sky over Rio. After that, once they had landed safely, came the seemingly endless questioning from the police, until they were suddenly allowed to go free.

She remembers Jay bringing her back to his apartment and, being the gentleman, allowing her to sleep in his bed while he crashed out on the sofa. It had been late morning by then, but Katrina was so exhausted, there had been no question in her mind that she would have difficulty in falling asleep. She doesn't even remember climbing into bed.

There is a knock at the bedroom door. Katrina pulls the sheet up a little higher. 'Come in.'

The bedroom door opens and Jay walks in, carrying a mug of coffee. He is wearing shorts and a T-shirt, and his face and left arm are covered in bruises.

He smiles. 'Hey, I thought you were never going to wake up.'

'Good morning.' Katrina stretches her arms out and yawns. 'Oh, I mean, good afternoon.'

'Here, I brought you a coffee.'

'Thanks.' Katrina accepts the drink and takes a small sip. 'You look terrible.'

'You don't look so good yourself.'

'What do you mean? I . . . ' Katrina touches her cheek with her fingertips and flinches at the pain. 'Have you got a mirror?'

'Wait there.' Jay goes and gets Katrina a hand mirror. She is shocked at the face she sees looking back at her from the glass. Her face is bruised, and she has a black eye. The bruising extends down her neck and disappears beneath the sheet.

'Stahl gave us both a real good going-over, didn't he?' Jay says.

Katrina thinks of the last moment she saw him, just before she pulled the ripcord. 'I know what you mean. He was a nasty piece of work.'

'Yes, he was. You certainly dealt with him, though.'

'I can't believe I did that to him. We should have tried to hold on to him, but instead I kicked at him until he let go. I killed him.'

Jay sits down on the bed. 'No, you're not allowed to think that way. It was him or us, Katrina. He was trying to take us with him. He wouldn't have let us open the parachute if he could've helped it.'

'I suppose,' Katrina says. She can see the sense in what Jay is saying, but still she feels an awful sense of responsibility.

'Here, put this on,' Jay says, handing her a dressing gown. 'There's somebody here to see you.'

Jay leaves the bedroom and Katrina pulls on the dressing gown. Since arriving at Jay's apartment, she guesses she has had about six hours of sleep. She needs more, but she's intrigued by the identity of her mystery visitor.

The living area is dominated by a picture window filled with sky and sea and distant mountains. Rising from his seat on the balcony, arms outstretched in greeting, is Everett McCluskey.

'Katrina, it's good to see you safe and well. You and Jay have been through an unimaginable ordeal.' He wraps his arms gently around her and gives her a peck on the cheek.

'Careful with the hugs,' Katrina says, flinching. 'I'm kinda sore right now.'

They sit on the balcony, the warm sun and the gentle breeze soothing her aching body.

'I'm sorry I haven't been able to see you before now,' McCluskey says. 'But I expect you have been grateful for the chance to sleep and rest.'

'You can't imagine,' Katrina says. 'But I still don't understand why the police let us go so quickly this morning. I mean, not only was there a dead policeman under my bed, but we had just crashed a plane and survived a 12,000-foot freefall. Not an everyday occurrence, even in Rio, surely?'

McCluskey smiles. 'My people got on to the police and, shall we say, encouraged them to let you go. We told them that we'll deal with matters from now on.'

'I've said this before, but I've gotta say it again: you're the strangest politician I've ever met,' Jay says.

McCluskey laughs. 'And, as I said before, I like to take a hands-on approach to the job.'

'How is Tom?' Katrina asks. 'Did he . . . ?'

'Tom's just fine. He lost a lot of blood, but he's in the hospital in a stable condition. We'll fly him back to the States as soon as we can. Knowing Tom, he'll be back on his feet and raring to go in no time.'

Katrina sighs and feels her body relaxing. 'Good. That's really good. Send him our best wishes, will you?'

McCluskey smiles and nods. He looks from Katrina to Jay thoughtfully. 'Looks like this experience may have had an unexpected, but rather pleasant, outcome for you two, am I right?'

Katrina reaches out and takes Jay's hand. 'Could be you're right, Mr McCluskey.'

'Please, call me Everett. Well, I just called by to see how you two were doing, and let you know a couple of things. First off, the police won't be bothering you with any more questions. US law enforcement is taking on the investigation from here, but I doubt they will be bothering you either. Secondly, we found Stahl, and recovered the USB device from him.'

Katrina sits up in her chair. 'Is he . . . ?'

'As dead as they come, Katrina, but don't you go feeling bad about that. Jay's already filled me in on what happened up there, and as far as I'm concerned, you deserve a medal. Stahl was a nasty piece of work, and the world's a finer place without him. As for Lowenstein's USB stick, well, that was a revelation. We found details of his invention and the design template, but something else too. Lowenstein had details of Coeus Petroleum's rather more, shall we say, murkier business contracts. The information we've now got on them, thanks to Lowenstein and you guys, will dismantle the company and send most of the management board to jail.'

'No wonder they were willing to employ a slimeball like Stahl to get that USB stick back,' Jay says.

'That's right. But the wheels of justice are already in motion, and they won't be operational for much longer.' McCluskey stands. 'Well, I'm not going to take up any more of your time. You both look like you could do with a good sleep. Keep an eye on the news over the next few weeks. You'll see some interesting developments.' He bends down and kisses Katrina lightly on the cheek, then shakes Jay's hand.

Jay sees the politician out. Katrina gazes out across the rooftops and at the sea in the distance. She feels peaceful and ready to go back to bed to catch up on some more sleep. After the stress of the last couple of days, and all the excitement, she feels like she could sleep for a week.

Jay returns, leans down and kisses the top of her head. 'Looks like this is your day for visitors.'

'Hey girl!' cries a familiar and welcome voice. 'What kinda crazy stuff have you been up to?' Quinn swaggers onto the balcony and gives Katrina a big hug. Katrina yelps, and then starts giggling. 'Oh, hun, I'm sorry.' Quinn steps back, seeing Katrina's bruises for the first time. 'He hurt you bad, didn't he?'

'Yeah, well, he won't be hurting anybody ever again,' Jay says.

'Now, I want to know everything that's happened to you two guys, but first I've got somebody here you're gonna want to see.'

Katrina turns in her chair and sees Enrique standing behind her. In his arms he is cradling a very contented-looking cat.

'Atticus!'

At the sound of Katrina's call, Atticus leaps out of Enrique's arms and runs over and jumps in her lap, immediately starting to purr. Katrina scratches him behind his ears and looks up at her friends. 'It's been a rough couple of days, but everything's going to be all right now,' she says.

* * *

Later that evening, Katrina and Jay are sitting on the balcony, drinking a glass of wine. The night sky is cloudless and, beneath the light of the full moon, Jay has been pointing out the stars and their constellations.

Now they are quiet. It is a companionable silence, one that seems like it might stretch out all night, until Katrina finally speaks.

'Hey, have you seen Atticus anywhere? I haven't seen him for a while.'

Jay smiles. 'He's curled up on my bed, fast asleep.'

'Oh no, I'm sorry. Do you want me to move him?'

Jay shakes his head. 'Nah, he looks like he's made himself at home there. Let's leave him. In fact, he's welcome to stay as long as he wants.' Jay pauses and looks at Katrina. 'You know, you're welcome to stay as long as you want, too.'

'Yes, I know,' replies Katrina, and she smiles. 'I think that would be nice.'

'Good.' Jay takes a sip of his wine. 'That's settled then.'

'Wait a minute,' Katrina says, sitting upright. 'You know what? There's still one thing about this whole mess that I don't understand.'

'Yeah? What's that?'

Katrina leans forward in her chair and points a finger Jay. 'You still haven't told me what J stands for.'

'I already told you, I'm not telling

you that. The only people who know that are back in Australia, and that's the way I'm keeping it.'

Katrina puts down her wine and stands up. She straddles Jay and sits on his lap, pinning him to the chair. She drapes her arms around his neck. 'No way, mister. I jumped out of a plane without a parachute to save you, so you owe me big-time.'

Jay sighs, but he is smiling. 'I guess I do. But you're not going to keep reminding me of that, are you?'

Katrina shrugs and kisses him lightly on the lips. 'I might, I might not.'

'You'd better not. If word of this gets out, my reputation as a tough guy will be in tatters. And nobody will ever trust me to take them skydiving again.'

'Don't worry, your reputation is safe with me. Now, come on, buster, spill. What is the J short for?'

Jay sighs. 'Justice.'

'What?'

'My first name is Justice.'

Katrina throws her head back and

laughs. 'No! You're kidding me, right?'
'I wish I was. My dad was a huge fan of this sixties cop show, *Justice Stone*. The repeats played on Australian TV all the time. Our surname was Stone, and so . . . '
'He thought he would call his son Justice?'
Jay screws his face up. 'Yeah. I've spent my whole life trying to live it down.'
Katrina kisses him again, a little longer this time. 'I think it's a fantastic name. I'm going to call you Justice from now on.'
'Don't you dare. I still bear the psychological scars from the teasing and bullying I got at school.'
'Oh you poor thing,' Katrina says, her lips brushing his.
They kiss a little longer, until Jay pulls back. 'Wait a minute. There's something I don't understand about this whole mess, either.'
'What's that?'
'These bruises going down your neck.' Jay starts tugging at Katrina's dressing

gown, pulling it apart. 'I think we should check how far they extend over your body. In fact, I think I should give you a thorough checking-out, all over. You never know where there might be some more bruises.'

Giggling, Katrina wriggles her way completely out of the dressing gown and lets Jay throw it on the floor. Pretty soon, she is checking him out for more bruises, too.

THE END